Scandalous

a novel

by

GWEN CANNON

G Publishing LLC
Detroit, Michigan

Edited by: Anthony Ambrogio

Cover Design: Plan1 Design & Graphics
                www.plan1productions.com
                info@plan1productions.com

Published by G Publishing, LLC
P. O. Box 24374
Detroit, MI 48224

ISBN 13: 978-0-9820002-9-8
ISBN 10: 0-9820002-9-4

Library of Congress Control Number: 2009900071

Printed in the United States of America

Acknowledgements

First and foremost, I thank my creator. He has given me knowledge, strength, wisdom, and the love and support of my family as I continue to use the gift that God has blessed me with. Thanks to my husband, James, words cannot express the support and motivation you give me to continue writing. You're my rock to lean on when I'm feeling like nothing is going right. You always come through. Thanks to my mother, Mary Collins; I'm blessed to have you in my life. You support me, no matter what I'm going through. I can always pick up the phone to call you, and just hearing your voice makes me feel better. Thanks to my sister, my friend, Lettice Crawford (and her husband, James). You are strong and beautiful. Your wisdom, spirituality, and strength ignite so much positive energy whenever I'm around you. I know you want nothing but the best for me. Thanks to Toyia Baker, one of the nicest, most giving person I have ever met. Your artistic skills are unbelievable; you have a gift, and I appreciate your kindness. Thanks to my stylist, Kim Tyler; I have so much love and the utmost respect for you. You are beautiful and strong, and you keep it real. Thanks for keeping my hair tight. Thanks to my family, who continues to support me: my brother, Aaron, and his wife, Lisa, in Atlanta; my sisters—Deborah, Rosemary, Rosilin, Margie (and her husband, Kevin Tabb); my nieces—Kesha, Catrea, Reese, Jessica, Kaela, Brandie, and Tosha; and my nephew, Lamar. Thanks also to the Cannon family—Fay, Delana, Bryan, and his wife, Crystal., and to the host of friends who continue to support me: Belinda Robinson, Emily Goodman, Gisela Estevan, Sam Garcia, Serena Levy, Ron Butler, E'lois Thomas; Carla, Salina, Darin, Chili, Mr. and Mrs. Tim Ford, DeAnna Stewart, Charles Crump, Tajuana and David Warren—not to mention my long-time family friends, whom I look up to as my big sisters, Yvonne Burge and Jackie Harvard. I would like to thank Coach Turner, Nollie, Ing, Sylvester, Mr. and Mrs. Kevin Beal, Juanita Lomax, William Lomax, Mr. and Mrs.

Robert Glimpse, Lisa Jones, Crystal Jones, Edith Maxwell, Diva, Christopher Loving, Lance Mason, P.C., and Bernadetta. A special thanks to my cousin out in L.A, recording artist, Une', the support you have given me is unbelievable. You put my book, "Stuck in the Dark" in someone's hands that may take it to another level and I thank you so much. I know I can't list everyone who has supported me, but please believe that I appreciate the support you all give me as I embark into the world of storytelling.

Chapter 1

Kesha

As I walked up my block, I kept wondering: Should I go home or should I turn my ass around and go back to my friend's house? Tell my girl another lie that my mother wasn't home and I couldn't get in? I didn't feel like seeing another one of momma's many male companions stretched out on our living room couch, holding the remote with one hand and scratching his crotch with the other. I hate seeing that shit.

Good, it's dark in the house; maybe they are asleep. Oh, hell naw—don't tell me I walked in on this kinda shit! My hoe-ish-ass momma is having a fucking threesome. Here she is, sucking a nigga's dick, while the other nigga is fucking her from behind. Now, that's some foul ass shit.

"Mom, Mom!" I hollered.

"Damn, baby girl, you want to join us?" smiled this old-ass man, grabbing and pinching my mom's breast while she was giving him head.

"Hell naw, old' motherfucka!" I screamed.

My mother raised her head just enough to tell me to go in my room and close the door. I couldn't believe this shit-she was acting like ain't like nothing happened. That's why I hated coming home to this motherfucka; I never knew what I was going to walk in on. I took my ass right back out the door.

It was nine years ago today my father walked out on us. My mom said that he couldn't handle a real woman. I think it was her hoe-ish ways that ran him off. I can remember many days when I caught my mom with other men while my dad was at work. She always claimed that she was doing it to do her part to bring money in the house. How can someone be so disrespectful? She was disrespecting her body as well as her home.

Gwen Cannon

She always used to tell me that I would never be broke as long as I had a pussy, used it, and got paid. Now—help me out people— ain't this shit something a ho' on the streets would say? My mom recommended it to me and my sister like it was as natural as getting your hair done.

"Use that shit until you can't use it no more, and don't worry about whose feelings get hurt in the process. Your pussy is like a bank account. Tell the nigga, if he wanna to make a deposit in the pussy, he gotta pay the transaction fee." My mother was a cold bitch who didn't give a damn whose feelings she hurt, as long as she got paid.

Now that's some nasty-ass shit. I don't want my pussy all tore up before I get twenty-one. I'm only seventeen and still a virgin, believe it or not.

To this day, my aunt won't speak to my mother. She caught my mom giving her man head in the garage. We were at my aunt's for a BBQ. My aunt went looking for my mom, and she walked in on them right in the act. My aunt beat the shit out of them. Momma gained a lot of bruises and lost her sister's love, all for the measly $20.00 dollars the guy promised her and never paid—the shit wasn't worth it.

I made a promise to myself not to turn out like my mother, but my sister—that's another story.

Flash money her way, and it's on and poppin'. Like mother, like daughter. I have bigger plans for myself. I want to become an attorney. I know it probably sounds impossible, considering my family history. But that's not going to stop me. I have always been strong minded. I don't let nobody talk me into doing shit I don't want to do, especially if it's some illegal shit. Hell naw, fuck that. I have sat back and planned out my future. Once I graduate next year, with a full scholarship, it's on and poppin'; I'm not going to let nothing get in the way of my dreams. As long as I maintain my 4.0, I shouldn't have a problem getting my scholarship.

Damn, here come this nigga Raheem. He's the biggest hoe I know, trying to fuck every female on the block. Just because he drive a BMW and is the biggest dope nigga on Linwood, that shit don't mean nothing. I hope his ass don't start asking me about my sister. I know she probably fucked the nigga. She got a good-ass job working at Macy's as a buyer. I can't understand why she wanna be up in this nigga face.

She has the book smarts, but, when it comes to niggas, she dumb as hell. No street sense. I don't understand. We grew up in the ghetto. I have to say, my mother might be a hoe, but she is street savvy. Niggas can't run game on her; she's the best at that. She can talk a nigga out of his fucking drawers—that's how good she is. Nigga can be ugly as hell; after my mother start spitting her game on a nigga, she make the nigga think he's the finest motherfucka in Detroit.

"What-up, Kesha?' asked Raheem, walking up smiling, showing his white gold grill.

"Shit," I muttered, frowning.

"Why you always acting like you have a fucking attitude?" asked Raheem.

"Look, Raheem, you don't want shit. You just looking for some free pussy"

"Damn Kesha, why you so hard on a nigga?" asked Raheem looking like he wanted to smack me.

"What do you want? I ain't got all day," I told him, folding my arms across my chest.

"Where your sista at?"

"How the fuck I know?

"You ain't gotta be all smart and shit"

"Raheem, like I said, how the fuck do I know where she at? Call her; go check her job. Damn!"

"Okay, Kesha, I'm going to leave your smart ass alone this time. That mouth of yours gone get you in a whole lot of trouble. I might have to put my dick in it just to shut you the fuck up." He grabbed his crotch as if to emphasize the point.

"That'll be the last time you stick your dick in anything. I will cut that motherfucka off."

"You know what? I'm gone let you slide on that one. You lucky you Nina's sister."

Raheem got on my fucking nerves. I couldn't stand him. I wish my sister would leave him the fuck along, before she get caught up in some shit. *I don't need a nigga to take care of me. I'm going to find me a job before the summer is over. I need new clothes for school and school supplies. I think I'll ask Raheem's brother, Jamal, if he can put in a word for me down at his office for a part-time summer job.* Jamal was Raheem's total opposite. Jamal was cute, smart and seemed to be a real gentleman. I wish he was into younger women; I would definitely holla.

I've always liked older men as long as I can remember. My first boyfriend was five years older than me. He went off to college, and that

Gwen Cannon

was the end of our relationship. I knew it wouldn't last, once he left. I wasn't surprised. I thought it was maybe that we hadn't had sex either. I told him I was saving myself for marriage. He would tell me to stop trying to live a fairy-tale life. To me, it's not a fairy tale; I have morals about how I want to do things, and having sex just because I have a boyfriend is not what I want.

Making love is special, and it shouldn't be with just any nigga you calling your boo. I have to feel some kind of spark or even a twitch between my legs. But so far, I haven't felt any of that. Damn, I'm up here daydreaming and shit, I better get my ass over to Jazmine's house before she leaves for the mall. If she's gone, I'll be waiting all fucking day.

Chapter 2

Jamal

*D*amn, *I could have sworn I put my gun under the car seat last night when I got home. Shit, I hope Ebony-ass ain't been up to her usual shit, playing games again.*

"Ebony, Ebony!" I hollered.

"Why the fuck are you hollering, Jamal? I hear your ass," said Ebony, coming down the stairs, rubbing her swollen round belly.

"You seen my gun?"

"Naw."

"Don't play with me; I need my piece!"

"Ask that broad you were with last night," smirked Ebony.

"What broad?"

Gwen Cannon

"Jamal, I heard your ass last night, screaming and shit. 'Fuck me, fuck me'" laughed Ebony.

"Oh, your nosy ass was listening?"

"Shit, you so fucking loud, I couldn't help but hear."

"You just jealous 'cause you can't get none."

"Oh, you got jokes? I can get dick any time I want to. You never had pregnant pussy, have you, Jamal?"

"Hell naw. What do I want with pregnant pussy when I can get any pussy I want?" I smiled, looking Ebony up and down.

"You know you want to try it."

"Girl, you my brother Chuck's woman; you need to quit with all that fucking playing around."

"Who said I was playing?"

"You know what—you a straight-up hoe, Ebony."

Ebony started taking off her clothes right in the living room. Even though she had a swollen belly, she still had an hour-glass figure. The pregnancy gave her a glow. I kept trying to look away, but my manhood wanted to see more.

"Ebony, you need to put your clothes back on. Why are you doing this shit? You know Chuck would swoop your ass if he found out."

"Jamal, look at me."

Ebony was butt-ass naked. She started rubbing her nipples and sucking on her finger. She put that finger between her legs. Then she sauntered over to me and starting rubbing my manhood. I was hard as a rock; I grabbed her breasts and starting licking and sucking on them. Before long, I dropped my pants around my ankles and let my erect dick wave free.

Ebony eased me down on the floor, mounted my dick, and slowly starting riding me. I caught the erotic rhythm of her movements and rocked with her. Before long, we were both sweating and panting like two dogs in heat.

"God damn, Ebony! Your pussy is hot as hell! Damn, it feels good!"

My body shook with spasms as I felt myself jerking to an explosive orgasm. "Oh shit, yes, yes, *yess!*" I hollered, as Ebony's cum ran down on me.

I guess Ebony was right about a pregnant woman and sex. That shit felt good as hell, it was hot, moist, and got a nigga hollering.

But then I sobered up.

"Damn, what the fuck have we done?" I asked, panting, getting up off the floor.

"Nothing, just sex between two adults," smiled Ebony, strutting around the room naked.

"Ebony, this can't happen again. Damn, I feel guilty as hell; you're my brother's woman, and you're pregnant."

"Jamal, don't feel guilty; it just happened."

"No, it didn't 'just happen.' You knew what the fuck you were doing."

"You sure wasn't trying to stop me."

"Just stop, Ebony, please. I don't need to hear that shit now. And put on your damn clothes."

"It's been four months, and I have wants and needs too. My hormones were calling for some dick; that's why my pussy was so hot. I needed to cool that shit off. Jamal, I know I shouldn't have let this happened, but we can't take it back. What's done is done. We both have to live with this shit. —Let's just act like it didn't happen," said Ebony, putting her clothes back on.

"I made a promise to my big brother Chuck that I would look out for you until he's home from basic training, and look what just happened!"

"Forget it, okay, Jamal? Quit tripping on that shit. You know Chuck loves the hell out of you and me. Let's just let it go."

"Shit, if that's love, I don't want it. Look what we did."

"Fuck you, Jamal."

"You just did."

"I could have had you a long time ago, but I chose your brother over you. He knows how to take care of a woman"

"Woman'—is that what you call yourself? Shit, a real woman would have a job and her own place. You just fucked me, so, if you are the image of a real woman, then the men in the world are fucked. I knew that's why your ass hooked up with Chuck. See he's too fucking soft when it comes to a pretty face. Nigga don't know how to man up."

"Whatever, Jamal. You wasn't saying that shit ten minutes ago. You was moaning and calling out to God."

I remained silent, staring at her.

"Yeah, I thought that might make you shut the fuck up," she said. "Drop me off at my cousin's house on your way to work. I think I'm going to stay over at her place for a couple of days. We both need some space after what just happened."

"Yeah, I agree, we need some space."

But I guess she didn't like the hangdog look on my face. "Just act like it never happened. *Damn!*" shouted Ebony.

"How am I going to look my brother in the eye after this?"

"Don't worry about it; just let it go."

Her anger overwhelmed me. "Okay," I capitulated. *Dawg—this bitch is something else. I'll try to let it go.*

With that settled, to Ebony's satisfaction, anyway, she changed the subject. "Jamal, can I ask you a question?"

"What, Ebony"

"Why do you carry a gun to work?"

"For protection."

"What kind of protection do you need at work? Don't you have security?"

"Yeah, and why are you asking so many fucking questions?"

"Just curious."

"No, just nosy as hell."

"Fuck it, Jamal; just drop me off. I'll be sure to mind my own business from now on."

Shit, six months is too damn long to be dealing with this airhead bitch Ebony. I don't know if I can take another two months of her in my house. Then I let this shit happen—and the thing about it is the shit felt good as hell! Yeah, I need her away from the house for a couple of days.

She can be sweet some days, but other days she can be a real B-I-T-C-H. The last four months have been a living hell, I don't know how my brother put up with her smart-ass mouth. I am proud of my brother for standing up and taking responsibility and leaving that drug game alone, doing something positive with his life before he got caught up or dead. I guess her getting pregnant changed him. But her being pregnant here is sure as hell changing me!

....

Damn, somebody's been on my computer.

"John, did anybody go in my office?" Jamal called from behind his computer screen.

"Yeah, the new girl—what's her name? I think Capri," said John.

"What the fuck was she doing in my office?"

"I don't know, bro, but I saw her go in there earlier today," said John.

"I'm gonna check this shit out." I got up and walked toward the reception area.

I stopped before her desk. "Excuse me, miss."

"Yes?" Capri looked up.

"I was informed that you were in my office earlier." I tried to look serious, but her hazel eyes caught me off guard.

"I apologize. I should have waited until you were here. I had no right to enter your office without your permission."

"Is there something you were looking for?"

"Some documents Mr. Cain needed for this morning's meeting."

"What documents?" I asked, trying to mask the worried look on my face.

"He said that you normally present the month-end budget report," said Capri.

"Is that what he told you?" I squinted suspiciously at Capri.

"Yes, but, when I looked where he instructed me to, I didn't see anything."

"Nothing for you to worry about. I'll get those reports to Mr. Cain." I turned to walk away, preoccupied.

"Hold up, Jamal," said Capri catching up to me. "I can take the reports to Mr. Cain."

"Okay," I agreed. But...

Something doesn't sound right; when have I ever reported out on the month end budget? Sounds like some shady shit is going on. I've had my suspicions for a while that somebody was trying to set me up to get fired, but I can't point the finger at anyone in particular. I hope it isn't Mr. Cain because I got so much dirty shit on his ass I could have him paying me hush money. But I have my own agenda on the table. I've been working for this company for nine years, producing the best results when it comes to bringing in new business, but I keep getting passed over for promotions every time for some motherfucka with a degree.

I ain't hatin' because of the degree; it's my fault I dropped out of school once I was hired in permanently. I should have kept my ass in school, and graduated. I only had one year to go. But, all I saw was dollar signs. Shit, I thought I had it made; I finally had a legit job. What I still can't understand, my boy John doesn't have a degree, but his ass got a promotion last month.

I wonder whose dick he's sucking, or, more likely, who he's letting fuck him in the ass. John's my boy, but his ass be sucking up to Mr. Cain, and I definitely ain't kissing nobody's ass just to get a raise or promotion. My work history and perfor- mance should be enough.

I better check in on my brother Raheem. I hope he took care of that business I asked him to do. His ass is so damn busy out there hustling them streets, he probably forgot what I asked him to do. I'm going *to need that information quicker than I thought. If my plan works out, I can retire at the ripe ol' age of thirty.*

Chapter 3

Kesha

"Can I speak to Nina Richards please?" I asked the operator, who connected me.

"Nina Richards speaking. How may I help you?"

"Hey, big sis, that asshole Raheem is looking for you," I said , giving her some attitude.

"What did he want?" asked Nina.

"Probably wanted to set up a fuck date." I didn't hide the sarcasm in my voice.

"Kesha, I'm busy. Is that all you called for?"

"Naw, I wanted to know if you could loan me some money until I get my first paycheck."

"You don't even have a job. Tell momma to give you some money, I gave her three hundred dollars yesterday," said Nina.

"Now, you already know she probably spent the money on some wine and who knows what else."

"Okay, Kesha," Nina sighed. "How much?"

"Two hundred dollars."

"*Two hundred*—damn! You lucky I love your ass. Meet me at 5:30, in the parking lot," said Nina

"Thanks, big sis. Love ya." I smiled into the phone.

"Yeah, whatever. Kesha, you love me when you know you're about to get something," laughed Nina

....

Damn, what's taking Nina so long to come out? It's almost 6 o'clock. Her car is still in the parking lot. I'm going to check with the front desk and see if she's still at her desk.

"Excuse me, I'm here to see Nina Richards," said Kesha.

"I'm sorry miss, but she left for the day at 4 o'clock," said the receptionist

"Do you know if she left a package or message for Kesha Richards?"

"No, ma'am"

I can't believe she just up and left and didn't even call to let me know she was leaving early. Wait until I catch up with her; I'm going to cuss her ass out. She probably left to go meet Raheem; I wouldn't be surprised. Let me call her cell phone. …Nina, answer the damn phone—it's going straight to her voice mail. I'm going to leave a message anyway.

"Nina, that's fucked up, what you did. You knew you were supposed to meet me in the parking lot at 5:30, and your ass just up and left and didn't call to let me know. Like I said, that's fucked up, but you'll need me someday Nina. You can bet on that."

I stormed out the building, mad as hell. *Now what am I going to do? I don't want to go home and ask my mother for shit. We'll just end up arguing as usual. I know by now that Jazmine is probably gone out hanging at the mall. I'm going to try her on her cell phone.*

"Jaz, where you at?" I asked when she answered.

"At Terrell's house" said Jazmine.

"What time are you coming home? I wanted to know if I can stay over tonight. I don't feel like seeing my moms."

"Kesha, your ass know you don't like going home; why don't you move in with your sister?" asked Jazmine

"That wouldn't work; she's all into that nigga Raheem. Who's probably fucking any and everything with a hole," I told her.

"I don't understand your sister. She's smart as hell, yet she loves living in the thug life. But I can't hate on her. Because I love a thug nigga too," said Jazmine laughing.

"That's cool and all, but, damn, why she have to be all into Raheem? He's scandalous as hell. If I offered him some pussy, that nigga would jump all over it, and wouldn't respect the fact that I'm her sister," I explained.

"Yeah, I believe that. I saw him yesterday trying to holla at Asia," said Jazmine.

"Asia's straight; we went to elementary school together. She can sing her ass off. I heard she might have a single coming out soon."

"Well, all I know is that I saw Raheem all up in her face," said Jazmine.

"He probably trying to holla to see if he can get some new pussy."

"Yeah, you're probably right. If I was your sister, I would be careful around that nigga. I don't trust him. I heard he like to beat his women" said Jazmine.

"Shit, I wish he would put his hands on my sister. That nigga would definitely be a ghost around here!" I vowed.

"Damn, Kee, your ass know you don't be playing when it come to your family. I'm glad I'm your friend and not your enemy," said Jazmine.

"Girl, you know I wouldn't do nothing to my home girl. You've always had my back since fifth grade. Remember my first day at Duffy Elementary? This big-ass bully name Bianca pushed me out of my chair, saying that I was in her seat. Your ass came up behind her and knocked the shit out her in the back of her head. Her big ass fell face forward on the floor. That shit was funny as hell, and we've been friend ever since."

"Yeah, that shit was funny. Your ass don't forget shit," laughed Jazmine. "I'll call you when I get home; you can come over for the night."

"Don't take too long, I'm hungry as hell."

"Girl, take your ass home—at least get something to eat. You act like you hate your momma," said Jazmine.

"I don't hate her; I just hate the shit she do. She don't act like the average mother should. In my eyes, my mother is a hoe."

"Damn, girl, you don't be holding shit up. Well, go home, pack a bag, and get something to eat. I'll call you," said Jazmine.

"Okay, I'll see you later."

Chapter 4

Malik

"Where the fuck is Raheem with my money?" I demanded.

"Malik, I talked to him about two hours ago. He said he would be here," Darius answered.

"That nigga better not try and fuck me over. I knew I shouldn't have started doing business with him. Nigga look shady as hell."

"I heard he was the go-to nigga when it comes to promoting your product," said Darius.

"Yeah, whatever, but I still don't trust his ass. Darius, call that nigga and see what's the hold up."

"Okay."

I've been in this business too long. I'm getting too old for this shit. I should have followed my mind and got out a long time ago, but greed took over. I wanted to have the best of both worlds. Now I'm out here on the corner looking for a motherfucka. Shit, I have my boys for this, but this is too much money just to let anybody pick up. I said I was going to retire a month ago, but I couldn't let this deal go through without getting in on it. Sounded too good to pass up.

I've been hustling since I was ten years old. My mom and dad got strung out on this shit when I was eight. I vividly remember the day I came home and found both of them laid out on the living-room floor with a needle stuck in their arm. At the time, I just thought they were high, because I had come home many days and found them like that, still with the needle in their arm. I didn't realize they were dead until the next day when I got up for school and they were still in the same position. I went over and touched my mother; there was white foam coming out of her mouth, and she felt cold and hard. I called 911 and told the operator I thought my mother and father were dead.

I guess they had got a hold of some bad shit. I didn't shed a tear; I just packed my bag and caught the bus to my grandmother's and told her I found them dead. At first, she thought I was going to need therapy because I showed no emotion. I told her I was all right and that I was used to seeing them like that. To me, they were just sleeping. I made a promise from that day forward that I would never use drugs.

"Malik," hollered Darius. "Raheem's voice mail came on"

"Do you know where he stay?" I asked.

"Naw, I know he kicking it with some broad named Nina."

"Put the word out that I'm looking for that motherfucka," I ordered, my face hard with hate.

"Okay, boss."

"Call me soon as you hear anything, and I mean anything. This motherfucka must don't know me. I knew I should have followed my mind about this nigga!"

Chapter 5

Jamal

"Raheem, did you get that information I needed?" I asked into the phone.

"Yeah, bro," said Raheem.

"Can you meet me at JC's at 7 o'clock?"

"Jamal, I'm kind of busy taking care of some business right now. What about 8:30?"

"Damn, man! What you doing? Got your dick up in some broad's ass or pussy?"

"You know your little brother—got to handle mine," laughed Raheem.

"Who you with now?"

"Nina."

"Kesha's big sister?" I was shocked.

"You know Kesha?" Raheem sounded a

little shocked himself.

"Yeah. I think she got a little crush on me. You know how girls get attracted to older guys. I think it's cute, but she's too young. Every time I see her, she makes sure she gives me a hug and lets me know that I can take her out anytime."

"Shit, fuck that; I'll fuck her. I don't care how old she is. Every time I see her little ass, she always got some smart-ass shit to say," complained Raheem.

"Damn, man, you don't care who or what you stick your dick in, and—did you forget?— you're fucking her sister."

"Whatever, bro," said Raheem.

"Your ass better be careful out there; somebody gone fuck your ass up," I warned him.

"Yeah right. I'm handling mine."

"Just make sure you deliver my package. I really need that shit now."

"I got your back, bro. I took care of everything; you'll be happy with the results. Just wait until you see them," said Raheem.

"Yeah, I can't wait."

"Is Ebony driving you crazy, man? I can't even imagine living in the same house with her," said Raheem.

"Hell yeah, she's driving me crazy. She got a smart-ass mouth." I laughed, trying to sound nonchalant.

"I know Chuck can't wait to get home," said Raheem.

"Yeah, man, I'll be glad too. Our big bro got two more months."

"I'm surprised her wild ass just been chilling," said Raheem.

"Uh, probably because she's pregnant—ain't too much shit she can get into," I said.

"Chuck got one of his boys keeping an eye on her ass too," said Raheem.

"Who?" I asked, trying to keep the concern out of my voice.

"Larry. He kicking it with her cousin Jada."

"I dropped her ass off over there this morning."

"I wonder if Larry got any info on her ass," said Raheem.

"I doubt it," I said—maybe a little bit more quickly than I should have. "Lately she just been chilling at the house and shit."

"Well, if she's been up to some shit, Larry will know," said Raheem.

"Raheem!" I heard Nina holler in the background. "Bring your ass on. Damn—I've been soaking in the Jacuzzi for fifteen minutes.

Who are you talking to on the phone?"

"Take your ass back in the room; I'll be there in a minute," yelled Raheem.

"Man, it sound like somebody mad at your ass; you better go handle your business. I'll see you at JC's later." I hung up the phone.

Chapter 6

Kesha

"Mom, you home?" I called as I entered the house.

"Your momma went to the grocery store," shouted a familiar voice from the living room.

My footsteps froze in place; my mind was telling me it was my father's voice, but I didn't want to get my hopes up. I hadn't seen or heard from him in years. I tried to stay calm and slowly walked into the living room. There; seated on the couch was my father, looking the same. Just like the last time I saw him. Tears started forming in my eyes, I tried to hold them back, but they were flowing. I didn't know if they were tears of joy from seeing him or tears of hate because he'd left me with this woman.

"Baby girl, aren't you glad to see me?" asked my father, gesturing to me for a hug.

"Yeah, I guess…"

"Come here; let me take a look at you. You have grown up to be such a beautiful young lady. Tell me about yourself—what have you been doing? How's school" he asked excitedly.

"Straight," I said sarcastically.

"What kind of answer is 'straight'?"

Before I knew it, I just snapped. I started cussing and throwing anything I could get my hands on at this man. How in the fuck could he ask me how's everything. Did he really want to know the truth?

"Well, daddy, where should I start? By telling you that there's a different man laid up in here every other day? That I can't stand to come to my own house because I don't know who the fuck is going to be here? My life has been fucking hell since you left. I thought you were dead. No letters, no phone calls—what the fuck was I supposed to think daddy? Huh?"

"Baby, I'm so sorry. I acted selfishly. I wasn't thinking about anyone but myself when I just up and left. Your mother put me through so much hell—and you know I gave your mother all my love. But she didn't appreciate a good hard-working man. When I came home and caught her in bed with another man, I knew, if I didn't leave, I would have probably killed her. So I thought it was best if I just left. But that is no excuse for the way I did you and your sister."

"Daddy, why did you come back?" I asked, tears streaming down my face.

"Your mother got in touch with my sister and told her that she was on her dying bed and that she wanted to see me before she passed. Your mother hasn't changed. I couldn't believe it when I drove up and saw her on the porch, drinking a can of beer looking healthy as hell. I should have known something wasn't right. But I knew, once I got here, I couldn't leave without seeing my baby girl. I wanted to see you and your sister before I left."

"So, the only reason you came back was because you thought moms was dying. Not because you wanted to see your daughters?"

"Kesha, I'm sorry. I cannot say how sorry I am. I deserve everything you are saying."

"So, you're leaving again?"

"No, I'm just leaving this house, I can't stay here. Your mother hasn't changed, and I think she never will."

"Daddy, can I come live with you?" I asked hopefully.

"Baby, I have a new family now, and I will have to check with my wife."

"'Wife'? You're married? You never married my mother. Now you are married, with a new family. So you're telling me that I have brothers and sisters?"

"Yes, two brothers and one sister. Your brothers are twins, 7 years old, and your little sister is five. I can't wait for you to meet them."

"What makes you think I want to meet them?"

"I'm sorry, I thought you would be excited and would want to."

"'Excited,' 'excited'—I can't believe that you would even let those words come out your mouth! What the fuck am I supposed to be excited about, daddy? The fact that you came back? Or that I have two brothers and a sister? —You know what? Please leave. As far as I'm concerned, I don't have a father."

"Kesha, you don't mean that."

"Yes, I do." You've been gone nine years and couldn't wait to start up a new family. You definitely weren't thinking about Kesha."

"Look, I'll leave. I didn't mean to upset

you. Please, take my number. Call me if you need anything. I know I can't take back what has happened, but we can make a new start. I'm so sorry; you didn't' deserve any of this."

"Daddy, I don't mean to sound harsh, just get out."

As he walked out the door, the tears started flowing again. For joy? Or hate? Only time would tell. *I can't wait for my mother sorry ass to get home. I'm going the fuck off.*

Chapter 7

Malik

"**A**sia, did you pick up my clothes from the cleaners for me?"

"Yes, big brother," said Asia, smiling.

"Your single, sounds good. This might be your start, baby girl."

"I hope so, Malik. I love singing. Is it true that our mother could sing?"

"Yeah, she used to sing the hell out of that old-school music. But she didn't' put her talent to good use. That's why I'm making sure you use your voice. You sing like an angel, baby girl. —I'm glad your adoptive parents were good people and didn't try and stop me from seeing you."

"Yeah, I really miss them," said Asia.

"Well, they are doing what every senior citizen should be doing. Taking it easy and living in sunny Florida. I couldn't believe they had adopted you at their age, but I'm glad. They were straight."

"Yeah, I'm going out to visit them for Thanksgiving and Christmas—that's the least I can do. I'm glad you went and got legal custody of me. I know they were relieved," said Asia.

"Well, it was time for me to take care of my baby sister."

"Can you drop me off at the mall when you get ready to leave?" asked Asia.

"What you trying to buy now?"

"I need something fly to wear to my release party." Asia danced around the room.

"You're really excited about this huh?" asked Malik smiling.

"Yes, I can't wait" said Asia.

"Go on and get dressed; I'll call you when I'm ready" said Malik.

"Okay," said Asia.

....

I better check with Darius and see if he heard anything. I can't wait until I see that motherfucka Raheem. He better hope and pray that the angels are watching over him, because, if this nigga has tried to fuck over me, he's dead.

I decided to call Darius. "Darius, what up?"

"Raheem said he got your package, but you'll have to wait until tomorrow," said Darius.

"What the fuck he mean by 'tomorrow'?".

"I don't know, man, but that's what he told me over the phone. I tried to find out where the nigga was at, but he kept trying to change the subject," said Darius.

"That's all right. I can wait until tomorrow. But, if that motherfucka don't have my shit, he dead!"

"Man, I'll holla back later," said Darius.

"All right."

Chapter 8

Jamal

"Hell naw" I laughed.

"You mean ol' boy was cool?" asked Raheem.

"Yeah, damn John sucking on some dick to move on up," I said, laughing, looking at the video.

"You owe me big time, bro; you lucky I love your ass. Because I could have got paid big time for some shit like this."

"Damn, I don't know how I'm going to act when I see John tomorrow at work. This shit is funny as hell," I said.

"Well, bro, I love you, but I gotta go. I got some business I got to take care of," said Raheem.

I sat at the bar laughing to myself. I couldn't believe the shit that was captured on the video recorder. I got shit I wasn't even trying to record. Different broads in the office fucking Mr. Cain, along with other employees. *Damn, I could blackmail a whole lot of motherfucka's if I wanted to. I didn't know my brother had his boy set up a video in the closet. Shit, motherfucka's was doing quickies in the closet. The new girl got her ass broken in quick. She just started a week ago.*

I wonder what Ebony is doing at her cousin's house. I don't even know why she crossed my mind. I got to get that shit out of my system. Just remember Ebony is my brother Chuck's woman; she's pregnant; and that shit won't work. I got to put my thoughts on my original plan.

Something told me to start taking notes at work. I could feel the tension from everyone. If I was going to get fired or set up, I definitely knew I would need something I could fall back on to cover my ass. I knew something was up when I started seeing different women employees going into Mr. Cain's office and then coming out twenty and thirty minutes later, smiling and shit.

I knew what was going on. Ol' boy was fucking each and every one of them. That's when I put my plan into place. I'm from the streets, and I knew the hustler part of me would never leave. If I saw a good hustle and I knew no one could get physically hurt, it was on. Shit, I was getting passed over for promotions anyway, so why not put my own promotion in place.

Setting up the video camera in Mr. Cain's office was easy as hell. Stupid-ass nigga didn't even know. The camera was a little man holding a golf club, sitting front and center on his desk. I gave it to him as a gift for Father's Day, told the nigga he was a father figure, as well as a mentor to me. See how easily a nigga will fall for some phony shit like that. *I can't wait to show this shit to Mr. Cain, a nigga about to get paid. But I got to handle this shit carefully; I don't want it to blow up in my face. I got to sit back and think how I'm going to put this in place. I might need to involve another person to help—but who? Got to be somebody I can trust. Hmm…this is going to take longer than I thought.*

Chapter 9

Capri

I could feel the cum running down the side of my mouth. Here I was again on my knees giving another one of my many bosses head. But, I have to say the shit paid off every time. I let the nigga know up front, don't fuck with me on this. They already know from my demeanor that I'm ghetto as hell and will have a nigga taken care of if he tries to play me. I used to say I would never do this type of shit to get a promotion, but, at every company I have worked for, there are always several females who are either fucking the boss or giving him head on a regular basis. I always said I would never fuck my way up the corporate ladder, but, after seeing so many

Gwen Cannon

co-workers who were hired after me move on to better positions, I started doing what I had to do. Shit, fuck it. Who ain't fucking somebody up in this place? I found that out two days after I got hired.

I was walking past the maintenance closet, and I heard moaning. My nosy ass crept behind a cubicle and waited to see who was going to come out of the closet. Damn—my co-worker Lisa and….. oh, hell naw! The damn janitor. I know he has a tight body, but—*damn*, Lisa! I'm gone have to call ol' girl out on this shit. The first day I started working, she was bragging about shit. Her main line is, "I don't fuck a nigga for free."

I know for a fact that shit is a lie. I can tell by the clothes she wears. That shit she be wearing come from the resale shop on Drayton I just sat back and let her brag on herself to the other employees in our office. I wanted to call her ass out, but, seeing that I just started. I thought I'd just sit back and take notes on her hoe-ish ass. *At least get paid for that shit.* But, to each its own is my motto.

I let a nigga know this bitch is broke. I ain't trying to please nobody or make no friends. She been working here eight years from what I heard, and her ass still has the same position. I hope her dumb ass is getting paid for that shit. I just got here a week ago and just made $500 from sucking the boss's dick. I definitely will suck a dick dry for $500. I have my eyes set on some new shit in the office now.

Ol' boy Jamal. Nice looking brother. He looks so familiar, I know I've seen him before. It will come to me where I know him from. Maybe he was cool with my brother. Next time I see him in the office, I'll ask if he knew Ron from Dexter Street.

Gwen Cannon

Chapter 10

Kesha

I saw my mother coming up the walk and tried to stifle my tears. But seeing her only made them fall faster.

"Kesha, why you sitting out here on the porch crying?" she asked.

"You know goddamn well why I'm sitting here."

She got all up in my face. "Listen, little girl, who the fuck do you think you are talking to like that?"

"You *bitch!*" I hollered.

"Don't test me, Kesha. I can still swoop your ass!"

"I wish you would try."

"What did you say?"

"You heard me; I didn't stutter."

Before I could get another word out, my mother slapped the shit out of me. I retaliated and punched her in the stomach. She bent over and charged into me, throwing me back against the door. I pulled at her weave, holding on for dear life. I wanted to scratch her fucking eyes out. There was so much anger built up in me from past hurts that I wanted to kill her.

I could feel the blood dripping from my lip. I didn't care, I just wanted to fuck her up for fucking up my life. The neighbor next door just stood in her yard watching, like she was looking at some tv show. We were tussling, holding on to each other. I had her weave, and she was holding on to my shirt collar.

This guy walking past ran up and tried to pull us apart.

"Lady, let go of her hair!" he said.

"I ain't letting go shit!" I told him, pulling even harder.

"Please—do I have to call the police?"

"Hell yeah, because I ain't letting go of this bitch's hair!"

"Okay—well, will you let go of her shirt?" he asked my mother.

"Hell naw!" she averred.

"—Kesha," she told me, "I'm gone swoop your ass. You think you grown, I'm gone swoop your ass like you a bitch on the streets."

"I feel like a bitch on the streets living with you. I might as well be. I hate you, mom, I really do," I cried.

"'Mom'?" The man was astonished. I guess he didn't know he'd walked into the middle of a domestic dispute.

"You hate me?" my mother asked, as if the idea never occurred to her before. Maybe it hadn't. I swear, I could see tears forming in her eyes, and they weren't from me pulling her hair, either.

"Yes, I hate you," I told her. "I have been living in hell all my life. I don't even know how it feels to have a mother. I have practically raised myself since I was eight years old. When daddy left, you might as well have left. You didn't think about me or Nina—we raised ourselves!"

"Baby, I thought I was doing what I had to do for my children."

"By sleeping with every motherfucka that showed you some money?"

"I did it to take care of you and your sister."

"You could've got a fucking real job, mom. That's no excuse. —Then I come home and find daddy sitting here telling me that you made up some bogus shit about dying so that he would come home. You been doing scandalous shit as long as I can remember, mom." I guess the emotion made me weak because I loosened my grip on her weave.

"What can I say? I'm sorry." And she let go my shirt collar—to show her sincerity, I guess.

But I wasn't having it. "It's too late for that shit. You should've said that when daddy up and left. I can't blame him. If I had been old enough then, I would have left with him!"

This was more than our passer-by had bargained for. "Uh—y'all gone be alright?" he asked, backing away from us.

"Yeah," I told him. And he was gone. Probably to go tell his wife about the two crazy bitches he'd encountered.

"What we gone do now?" mom asked, slumping against the front door, obviously exhausted from our exertions.

I plopped, cross-legged, on the porch. "Mom, I'm tired. I can't take any more. I'm only seventeen, and I feel like I'm thirty. I don't even know how it feels to be a teenager. I have to fend for myself. I can't go to Nina; she's got her own life to live. I'm not her responsibility."

"Kesha, I can try."

"Try and do what mom?"

"Try and be a mother."

"For some odd reason, that's hard to believe."

"Kesha, I wasn't lying when I called your father and told him I was dying."

"Mom, you aren't dying. You look pretty damn healthy to me. Damn near kicked my ass."

"Kesha, listen to me. I *am* dying. The doctor said I only have four to six months to live. I've been having headaches for over a year. I finally went to the doctor, and they found a tumor near my brain. There's excessive swelling, and there's no way they can operate. The doctor said I waited too late to come in. If I would have taken my ass to the doctor when the headaches started last year, they could have caught it sooner. Now it's too late. The alcohol and drugs didn't help either."

"Mom, I don't know what to say."

"There's nothing you can say."

"Why didn't you tell me sooner?"

"I didn't want to burden you and your sister with my problems. I've already caused enough pain in your lives."

"Regardless, you're still our mother."

"I know."

"Mom, what do we do now?"

"Just pray, baby; just pray."

Chapter 11

Malik

"Asia, you gone be alright at the mall by yourself?" I asked her as she got out of the car.

"Yes, big brother Malik," she smiled. closing the car door.

"Call me, when you're ready."

"Okay," she agreed and went inside.

....

"Darius, where you at, man?" I asked into my cell phone.

"I'm at Booty Call," said Darius.

"Did you get with ol' boy?"

"Naw, man, but I think I know where he be chilling at. I'll holla back at you," said Darius. He seemed in a hurry to get off the phone.

"I'm on my way to Booty Call. I want to be with you when you catch up with that nigga!"

This nigga making me go back to my younger days. I used to fuck a nigga up over little shit. I have definitely chilled. Damn, traffic is a motherfucka on the Southfield Freeway. I'm going to get off at the next exit. I can take Ford road on down. I think I'll stop at Chili's and grab me something to eat before I go to Booty Call. I hope they don't have a long wait.

As I was waiting to be seated, I looked over in the corner—and there was that motherfucka Raheem.

Damn, just my luck. I'm gone make my way over to his table and see his reaction. I don't want to cause no commotion in public. I don't want to be getting locked up on a Friday. Shit, is that a female with him? Fuck it, I'm still going over there.

"What up, Raheem?" I greeted, nonchalant.

"What up, man? I know you're pleased with how I flipped your bundle," smiled Raheem.

"What are you talking about, man?"

"Hey, don't be lookin' at me like I'm crazy. I met up with your boy Darius earlier. He told me you told him to get the package."

"Darius met up with you?"

Raheem's expression seemed to say, *Why don't this motha know that already?* "Yeah man, I wouldn't bullshit you. I ain't trying to get on your bad side. Look, I can show you on my cell phone. It lists all the numbers received and the length of time. See, right there: that's Darius number. He called at 9:15 this morning, woke me up out of my sleep. Said that you didn't want to wait until later," said Raheem, pointing at the listed call.

"How much did you give him?" I was trying to stay calm.

"Five hundred thousand. I told you I would be able to double your money."

"That motherfucka played me!"

Everyone in the restaurant turned their attention to the man hollering in their midst. That's when I lost it. I started pounding on the table and shit. Raheem tried to grab my arm and calm me down, but I pushed him so hard he fell on the floor.

A restaurant employee came over and asked was everything alright. Raheem convinced them that everything was okay, that I was just a little upset.

"Malik, let's go outside man. We need to talk." Raheem pulled me toward the exit before the restaurant called the cops or something.

Out in the parking lot, Raheem cautioned me, "Malik, calm down. You know what you have to do. I haven't been in this game this long for nothing. I know we think we have niggas we can trust. That's bullshit; that's why I work alone. I learned that shit a long time ago. In this game, you can't trust nobody, not even your family. Every man for himself."

I stood there, fists clenched. I swear, no one could comprehend the anger that had built up inside me. I had heard every word Raheem said and knew it was the truth. I should never have let my guard down, no matter how long I'd worked with that fuckin' double-cross nigga.

Me and Darius went 'way back. Almost sixteen years. Darius was like a brother to me. We met after Darius ran away from his foster mother and father and clicked immediately. We had so much in common—the broken home, the mother and father strung out on drugs.

I felt I had finally met someone I could trust with my life. Darius proved his dedication over and over, like when he killed Big Mo, that upstart dealer who was trying to muscle in on my territory. He cut off Mo's pinky finger and gave it to me to show his loyalty. I thought

Gwen Cannon

back to what my grandmother used to tell me: money is the ruler of all evil. I could hear her words ringing in my ear.

"Are you gone be alright, man? Are we cool?" asked Raheem, looking nervous.

"Yeah, we straight," I told him.

"I can go with you, if you want me to," Raheem offered.

"I need to take care of this on my own." Raheem made like he was going to protest, but I guess the look of pure hatred on my face discouraged him from insisting. I left him there and started toward my car.

Chapter 12

Jamal, Capri, and John

*W*ho can I trust with this shit? I know a lot of scandalous motherfuckas that would jump to make some money. But I don't know— when money is involved, people you thought you could trust will turn on your ass in a minute. Hmmm, I wonder... Ol' girl came on board putting her shit on point. She was up in Mr. Cain's office giving helluva head less than a week after being hired. Shit, she might be the right person to bring in on this shit. I'm gone holla at her tomorrow to see where her head is at.

....

"Good morning, Capri," Jamal greeted, flashing me a big, bright toothpaste-commercial smile.

"Good morning, Mr. Long," I responded warily, wondering what was wrong with him.

Ol' boy must be feeling good this morning. This is the first time he acknowledged me in the morning. He normally just waves as he's walking by. I know I've only been here a little over a week, but I try to say good morning to everyone. Got to keep my happy-go-lucky reputation. I can't let niggas know the real me. If they did, my ass would be out the door. I know I do my dirty shit, but I don't hurt nobody. I just want to get paid and keep stepping. I've been waiting for my big pay day, but it don't look like it's coming too soon.

"Capri, when you have time, I would like to see you in my office for a moment." Same wolfish grin plastered on his shit-ass face.

"Okay, Mr. Long. I have to type a memo for Mr. Cain. Can you give me fifteen minutes?"

"That's fine. I'll see you then," he agreed.

....

Okay, now I have to come up with how to approach ol' girl with my plan. Should I just up and ask her? Or should I close the door and pull out the photos? Yeah, that's how I'm going to do it, let her ass know up front that I know all about her and Mr. Cain.

Just then, she buzzed me on the intercom. "Mr. Long, Can I come to your office now?"

"By all means," I said. I sat back and waited to spring the trap.

She knocked softly.

"Please come in and close the door behind you," I told her.

"What can I do for you?" asked Capri, looking nervous.

"Please, don't be nervous. Have a seat," I said, all smiles.

"Okay." She sat on the edge of the chair facing me, like she wanted to make a quick getaway.

I put on my most serious face. "I'm not going to beat around the bush or play games with you Capri, I called you in my office for a proposition." I waited for her reaction.

....

What's that serious smirk on his face supposed to mean? Damn, don't tell me this motherfucka want his dick sucked too. I didn't plan on sucking every dick in the office.

"What type of 'proposition'?" I asked, looking around the office, staring at the closed door.

He just smiled and handed me an envelope. I opened it, looked at the contents, then looked back at him. I wasn't smiling. "So, what the fuck do you want, Jamal?"

"Calm down, Capri, and listen."

"Okay, I'm listening," I frowned, folding my arms across my chest

"I can help you make a lot of money." He was smiling again.

....

Boy, that statement made her whole demeanor change. I even saw a slight smile creep across her face.

"What's involved in making all this money?" she asked.

"First, I need to know if I can trust you. I don't want to have to come looking for your ass. Right now, I trust you more than someone I personally know."

"So, are you going to tell me what I have to do?"

"Nothing you haven't already done," I said cryptically.

"I tried that blackmail shit before, and it backfired on me. I don't need you for that shit!"

"Naw, what I have planned will get me and you paid. I have more than just pictures and videos of Mr. Cain."

"Shit, I'm in, if it's going to get a sista paid." Now she was actually grinning.

"I have to put everything in place. I don't want no fuck ups. Everything will have to go as planned if we want this to work. I'll call you in a week with the full details. Just make sure you don't mention this shit to nobody—and I mean not one fucking person. I don't care if it's your sister, brother, homegirl. We are the only ones, Capri. I'm already putting myself out by letting you in on this shit. I just met you last week. But I peeped your ass, once I saw the pictures and the video. At least your ass got paid."

"I don't get on my knees for free. Fuck that," she told me.

"Well, now that we have a mutual understanding. I'll be calling you."

....

I walked out of his office with a big ass grin on my face. *Damn, my big pay day has finally come sooner than I thought. I was just complaining about this shit. Damn, I wonder what his plans are.*

"Oops, excuse me. I'm sorry, I wasn't paying attention." I looked up to see John, smiling down at me.

"No problem," he grinned.

"I hope your day is going well, and if I don't see you later have a nice weekend," I beamed in return.

"Same to you," he said, as I sashayed away.

....

I watched her hips sway under that thin dress on her way back to her desk.

Damn, ol' girl smiling like she hit the lottery. I saw her coming out of Jamal's office. I wonder what that was about. Shit, Jamal gone have to kiss and tell.

I knocked on his door.

....

"Come in," I said. Was ol' girl returning for a quickie?

But it was John. "What up, nigga?" he asked, giving me dap.

"Nigga, what you smiling about?" I asked.

"I saw ol' girl leaving your office smiling and shit."

"Oh, I told her that I would try and look out for her if I hear of any new positions in the company. I know she's only been here a little over a week, but she's very educated." I didn't want to give John any clue as to what was going on.

"Come on man, you can tell me. Did you hit that?" asked John, looking around the office for any clues.

"Nigga, didn't I tell you no?" I claimed, trying to sound serious. I didn't want to tell

John I knew all about him sucking Mr. Cain's dick.

"Okay, man, calm down. I know how every new chick be trying to rub up on you. You the man around here," smiled John.

"Yeah, whatever, nigga."

"You clubbing tonight?"

"Naw, I'm gone chill this weekend. I have some unfinished work to take care of."

I don't know why this nigga still in my office. It's taking everything in me not to call his ass out. Sucking Mr. Cain's dick. Damn John, I thought he was straight. He got a nice-ass woman, too. I bet her ass don't even know. Anything for a motherfuckin' raise or promotion. I guess if women can do it, so can niggas, but I ain't sucking a dick.

Now if my boss was a woman, shit, I'd fuck her ass, and eat her pussy too. I remember when I worked for Ranger Logistics. My manager was a woman--not the best-looking woman, but you could tell she must've been tight back in the day. Shit, she hooked a brother up. She told me to stick with her and I could go places in the company. I did just what ol' girl told me to do.

I know everybody was calling me a little bitch and shit, but ol' girl was tearing a nigga off swell. I would meet her after work every Friday. Put the

Gwen Cannon

dick on her strong and leave with a pocket full of money.

The only thing is I had to be her snitch. I didn't like that shit, but fuck it. Motherfuckas didn't care about me, so I told her what she wanted to hear, even if it was a lie. She believed every fucking thing I told her, I kinda felt bad, because a few people got fired. But I think the labor-relations manager had the hots for her ass too. This nigga would stare me down at every damn meeting. I wanted to tell his ass, "Nigga, she don't want your old ass." I better get my ass outta here early today, before Mr. Cain come up in here asking me to do some last minute shit.

"Alright man, have a good weekend," said John. I almost forgot he was there.

"You too, dog, —But how come you sayin' goodbye so early? Mr. Cain lettin' you take the rest of the day off? What you got on him, man?" I told him as he left.

He just gave me a shit-eating grin but finally left, faster than maybe he meant to. *I wonder why John is so fucking nosy.*

....

The rest of the day passed quickly, filled with the usual work and shit. Before I knew it, it was quitting time and I was outta there and off to my car.

I have a lot of thinking and planning to do over the next week if I want this shit to go through smoothly. That looks like Capri in the parking lot. What the fuck is John doing over there? Probably being nosy as hell again.

"Ms. Lady, I thought, when that whistle blows, that you're gone for the day," I told her.

"I'm on my way. John stopped me to ask about new positions in the company. I told him you were looking out," said Capri.

I see we think alike; she covered that shit up good. John still trying to find out shit. Look at his ass, like he got caught with a dick in his mouth. I knew his nosy ass was gone try and find out what she was doing in my office.

"'I'll make sure you get off okay," I told her.

"You're such a gentleman," she smiled.

"'Bye."

"'Bye, Mr. Long."

John and I stood there looking at each other. *I know he wants to ask me something but he already know I will cuss his ass out.*

"Are you happy now, John?"

"Naw, man, it ain't like that," said John.

"Whatever, man. I'm out," I said.

John stood in the parking lot as I drove off—a big smirk on his face, as if he knew what was going on between me and Capri.

Chapter 13

Kesha

"Nina, open the door."

"What's wrong? Why are you crying, Kesha?" asked Nina, looking at my tear-stained face.

"Momma!" was all I could say.

"What about momma?" asked Nina, looking worried.

"She's sick!"

"We know that. So what else is new?"

"Nina, I mean sick for real. She's *dying*!"

"Dying? What do you mean 'dying'?"

"She told me; she has a tumor on her brain, and there's nothing the doctors can do. They gave her four to six months," I said, wiping my eyes.

Gwen Cannon

Nina looked dazed, as if she didn't comprehend what I had just said. You could see the tears starting to form in the corners of her eyes.

"I know mom hasn't been the best mother in the world, but, regardless, she's still our mother. She brought us into this world. *I don't know what to do!*" cried Nina.

"We have to pray and make her last days here the best," I said.

"You seem so calm about this," said Nina.

"I cried all the way over here; you saw the last of it. I don't think I can shed another tear today. The long walk over here gave me time to think, and I realized that there's a reason for everything. Maybe God felt that it was her time, Nina; I don't know. All I know is that our mother won't be here long, and I want to make her happy. Oh—I forgot to mention: daddy's here, too." said Kesha looking for a response from Nina

I thought that would get a response from Nina, but she was still in deep thought about our mother. She wasn't grasping the additional news I'd just dropped in her lap. I could tell that all kinds of thoughts were running through her head. *Did momma hit her head on something? What causes a brain tumor?* Like me, when I first found out, Nina wanted answers; she wasn't accepting the fact that our mother wouldn't' be with us to celebrate Christmas or, in fact, any more holidays.

Nina finally came out of her trance and asked me about daddy showing up.

"Mom called dad and told him about her condition," I explained. "He didn't believe her."

"So, what was his excuse for leaving us?" asked Nina.

"Mom, of course."

"Yeah, I figured that," said Nina.

"I can't blame him. I have walked in on mom doing some shit I only thought they did in the movies," I told her.

"Well, I guess we better give him a call and let him know that mom was not lying," said Nina.

"Damn, I forgot to tell you! Me and mom had a fight," I mumbled, looking down at the floor, not wanting to see Nina's response.

"You *what*?" screamed Nina.

"I knew you would react that way; that's why I didn't want to tell you."

"She has a fucking tumor on her brain, Kesha!" screamed Nina

"I didn't believe her at first," I cried.

Gwen Cannon

"Okay, okay, we have to pull together now for mom. I know she wasn't the best, but she's our mother, no matter what."

"I know. Let's call dad."

Chapter 14

Malik and Asia

Driving to Booty Call gave me time to reflect back on my conversation with Darius. I should have paid more attention. He kept saying how he was about to go on a long-overdue vacation to Cancun. Shit, I just thought him and his girl was going out of town for a few days. He normally takes her on vacation with him every year. I never thought this day would come where I would have to make a decision to take my boy out.

I definitely can't let this shit just go. Damn, Darius, why did you have to go and do some shit like this? I would have given him some money—all he had to do was ask. Raheem made a good point when he said that you can't trust nobody in this

76   Gwen Cannon

*game, not even your family. Grandma was right —
money if the ruler of all evil. I should have gotten
out of this shit like I started to. Greed took over, and
I didn't want to pass up an opportunity to double
my money.*

My cell phone rang. "Damn, who the fuck
is this calling me now?"

It was Asia. "I'm ready; you can pick me up
by the entrance to Macy's."

"Can you wait about another thirty
minutes?" I asked her. "I have to make a quick
stop."

"Why don't you pick me up first, and I can
go with you?"

"No!"

"Okay, you don't have to holler. Are you
alright?" asked Asia, sounding concerned.

"Yeah, I just got to take care of something."

"Are you sure?" asked Asia getting
worried. I knew she thought that I might be
getting into something that might get me killed
or locked up. She knew, whenever I started
hollering, that it had to do with business.

"Yeah, baby girl, your big bro is alright." I
tried to sound calm.

"You know I got your back," said Asia,
trying to lighten up the conversation.

"I know; you my little row dog." I smiled, as if she could see my expression.

I love my little sister. I'd do anything for her. I would die for her. I always tell her, "If somebody says anything out of the way to you, just pick up the phone." She always imitates me, telling the same thing.

I was so deep in thought that I didn't notice the bright lights coming my way, head on.

I tried to swerve over to the other lane, but I was too slow. The truck hit the driver's side, sending my Range Rover flipping.

****

All I could hear was the rumble of a truck and about a million car horns blowing.

"Malik, Malik, what's wrong? What happened?"

I heard cars screeching to a stop. I knew something had happened to him. Tears started to swell up in my eyes, I was screaming into the phone, "Malik, Malik—please don't die; please don't die!"

Gwen Cannon

Chapter 15

Capri and Jamal

"Bitch about to get paid," I sang, dancing around my apartment.

My big payday has finally arrived. Ol' boy, knew who to go to. I'm making out a list of shit I want to do and buy. I need a new car — not that I don't love my BMW. Some new jewelry, another big-screen TV, a nice long-ass vacation, and a whole new wardrobe. Sister got to stay looking tight. Damn, is that my apartment buzzer going off? Who the fuck just showed up and didn't call? I hate that shit; I shouldn't answer the buzzer.

"Who is it?" I asked over the intercom.

"Jamal."

What the fuck is he doing here? I didn't give him my address.

I frowned. "How did you get my address?"

"Don't worry about that. Buzz me in. We need to talk."

So I did.

Motherfucka got my address, what else his ass been snooping around getting? I'm definitely going to check his ass about this.

"What's up, Ms. Lady" smiled Jamal coming in the door.

"How the *fuck* did you get my address?"

"Calm your ass down. I do have authorization to look at your employee file." He was still smiling.

I rolled my eyes. "Yeah, but you don't have authorization to show up at my apartment unannounced."

"I apologize; I should have called, but I wanted to get with you as soon as possible so we can plan this shit out."

"Okay, I'm ready." The thought of that big payday changed my mood for the better.

"Is anyone else here?" asked Jamal looking around her apartment

"No. Why?"

"Just want to make sure. I don't need any fuck-ups. I want this shit to go down smoothly without any interruptions."

....

I could tell she had expensive taste by the clothes she wore to work and definitely by her apartment. She had that shit laid out. I also noticed that she didn't mind showing off her body. She was wearing a pink tank top, with a matching thong. She wasn't' shy. I just sat on the couch watching her prance around the room cleaning up, grabbing a glass and empty pizza box from the table.

"Well, what's up? How we gone do this shit?" she asked, bending over right in front of me, giving me a full view of her ass.

"Are you going to put on some clothes?"

"No, I'm in the comfort of my home, and I feel relaxed in this. It ain't like you never seen a woman half naked. Do I make you nervous?" She smiled mischievously.

"Naw," I said, pulling at my shirt collar.

"Okay, then let's get this plan in motion."

"I want this to go down Friday," I said, watching her plan in motion.

I couldn't seem to concentrate with her parading around half naked. She came and flopped down on the couch next to me, rubbing her leg up against mine. I tried to scoot over a little. So did she.

She let her hand rest on my thigh and looked me directly in the eye. *Damn! I do feel nervous around her*. It was those hazel eyes that kept me glued to her. I could tell she worked out. Her stomach was flat as a pancake and showed off her tight abs. Capri started running her hand up and down my thigh. Ol' Mr. Long-in-My-Pants started rising. I knew she could see the outline of my dick, tenting my pants. *I* could see it (and feel it!). She was smiling. She knew exactly what she was doing. I put my hand on top of hers to stop her from rubbing.

She just looked at me with those hazel eyes again and took her other hand and laid it on top of my dick. That's when ol' Mr. Long-in-My-Pants took over and started doing the thinking for both of us.

I put my hand on Capri's breast and starting rubbing her nipples, making them hard. I pulled her tank top up and began sucking on her breast. She spread her legs and started rubbing her pussy. This turned me on even more. I pulled at her thong, and put my finger between her legs, rubbing her pussy. It was moist and wet. I stood up, pulled my pants down, picked Capri up from the couch, and put her directly on top of my dick. Holding her by the ass, I pounded my dick into her pussy while she wrapped her legs around me for support.

I stuck my tongue in her mouth. She started sucking my tongue so hard I thought she was going to bite it off. She could feel my orgasm coming on strong. I tried to hold back, but I couldn't.

We exploded in unison, each screaming in our own heat of passion. Cum was running down my leg from my climax and Capri's. We were panting like two dogs in heat, still holding on to each other, feeling that last moment of ecstasy.

....

Jamal and Capri didn't notice me looking through her blinds, but I sure as hell saw them. I stepped away from the window and started walking down the street.

Chapter 16

Kesha

"Nina what are you going to say to daddy?"

"I don't know. 'Where the fuck you been?' probably," laughed Nina.

"We have two brothers and a little sister," I informed her.

"What—this motherfucka got a whole new family?" asked Nina.

"Yep."

"Well, we can't be mad at the kids, but his ass is scandalous. Ran the fuck out on us and got a fresh start," said Nina.

"What was the name of the hotel he said he was staying at?" asked Kesha

"I think he said the Troy Inn. I wasn't trying to hear shit else he was saying on the phone," said Nina.

"Well, he is our father. I cussed his ass out too." Said Kesha smiling

"He deserved it. If momma wouldn't have called him, I guess his ass would still be gone," said Nina.

"I guess it wouldn't hurt to meet our brothers and little sister…" said Kesha

"Yeah, they are innocent. It's not their fault daddy fucked up," said Nina.

"There's a parking space over there," I pointed to an empty stall.

"Call his ass. I don't want to go up to his room. We can talk outside," said Nina.

"Daddy, we're outside in the parking lot…. No, Nina doesn't want to come up." I turned to Nina. "He's coming down now," I said–and couldn't help laughing at her.

"That shit ain't funny, Kesha," said Nina.

"I'm laughing at you; your ass is mad for real."

"You was mad too. You've just cooled off."

……………………………..

"How's my two favorite daughters?" asked daddy, smiling, walking toward us.

Nina just stood there, but I gave in and met him halfway, hugging him.

"I don't understand why you're here," said Nina.

"Your mother called me," he said.

"Yeah, whatever," said Nina sarcastically.

"Let's go get something to eat and catch up on old times," I suggested, trying to break the tension in the air between Nina and my dad.

"I'm not hungry," said Nina.

"Get something to drink then," I stated.

"I ain't thirsty, either," said Nina giving daddy a grim look.

"Nina, I know you are angry with me, and you have every right to be mad. I can't undo what has been done. I can only move on from here. Words cannot express how sorry I am. There's no explanation for what I did," he said.

"Daddy, you don't understand the hell we've been through since you left," said Nina.

"Kesha told me."

I stayed back and let Nina and daddy talk.

Even though I'm upset with him, I still love him. I understand why he had to leave—but he didn't have to leave from our lives completely. We needed the love of our father to get us through. If it wasn't for Nina having my back, I don't know how I would have turned out.

I turned around to see Nina and daddy hug.

"I guess we can go out to eat now," I smiled.

"Yes, little sister," said Nina, hugging me. She was full of hugs all of a sudden.

We piled into Nina's car and drove off to Red Lobster. We talked like old times, about daddy's new family and how he wanted us to come visit to meet his wife. We agreed that, from that day forward, we would definitely keep in touch and that we'd meet at least once a month for dinner. Daddy didn't live that far away; he had moved to Toledo, Ohio.

On the drive back to the hotel, I made daddy promise to bring our brothers and sister next weekend so that we could meet.

Chapter 17

Malik and Asia

I was aware of sirens in the distance, getting louder, and cars on the side of the road, all pointing *down* for some reason. That's 'cause the Range Rover lay on its side, with me in it. I seemed to be covered in this wet, red stuff. A bunch of faces sprouted at the windshield. They were all talking, but they sounded far away.

"Is he breathing?"

"Yes, but he's in bad shape."

Poor guy. I wonder who they're talking about?

Some guy in a fireman's helmet pushed away the faces. "Please stand back, we are going to have to cut the door off in order to get him out."

I heard a hissing sound, and everybody was talking at once.

"They had to call the fire department because, when EMS arrived, they couldn't' open the door."

"They have to use a blow torch to get the door open."

Oh. It's a blow-torch making that hissing sound, I understood.

The door, which had been above my head, disappeared, replaced by a bunch of guys in white, grabbing at me.

"He's in bad shape."

"Looks like his legs were crushed under the steering column."

"Is he conscious?"

"Sir, can you hear me?"

"Yeah. What's the problem?" I asked. "I need to be going someplace—"

"He's conscious, but he isn't aware of the damage he's sustained. —Just lie still, sir, and we'll take care of you."

I was gonna get up anyway, but I discovered that all I *could* do was lie still.

They lifted me up and out of the Range Rover, onto some stretcher.

"Please stand back," the medic gestured to the crowd.

Then we were in the ambulance. It was making a helluva racket as it zoomed off.

"Take him to Riverside emergency. It's closest."

....

I was kinda awake and not awake for a long time. Before I knew it, we weren't traveling by ambulance anymore. I was on one of them guernies like they use on the doctor shows on tv.

"Does anyone know his name?" asked a nurse, running alongside my moving cart.

"His wallet is in a bag with his personal items. Take a look at his cell phone," said the medic.

Hey, that's my personal property! I was going to tell them, but I was too tired to talk all of a sudden.

I saw the nurse scroll through my call list. She must've seen that Asia was the last person I talked to. Anyway, she dialed some number.

....

Asia was worried—the last time she talked to Malik, she could hear screeching. It sounded like an accident. She could hear people hollering for help. She couldn't get him back on his cell phone. Damn, Malik's calling now. I hope he's alright.

"Malik, is that you?"

"No, this is Nurse Smith calling from Riverside Hospital; may I speak to Asia?"

"This is Asia."

"Are you related to Malik Waters?"

"Yes, I'm his sister!" I cried.

"He's been in an accident. He's at Riverside Hospital, located across from Fairmount Mall in Dearborn," said the nurse.

"I'm on my way!"

What the hell happened to Malik while we were on the phone? God, please take care of my brother. He's the only real family I have besides my foster parents.

I waved down a cab and went directly to the hospital. When I arrived, I was faced with the news that Malik's legs were crushed and they were trying to amputate them.

I advised them to do everything they could to save his legs. *Malik would die if he knew they were even considering cutting off his legs.*

Waiting for Malik to come out of surgery, it seemed like a whole day had passed. Finally, I saw the Doctor coming my way.

"Asia Waters?" he asked.

"Yes?"

"We were able to save his legs. However, it's going to be a long, extensive recovery process. We had to put metal screws and pins to help mend his legs."

"I don't care how long it takes. Thank you, Doctor. When can I see him?"

"He's in recovery, he'll be moved to intensive care shortly. You can see him once they take him to his room. He probably won't know you're there. He's heavily medicated."

"I don't care; I'm not going anywhere."

I better call Darius, I wonder if he know what happened. He's going to be tripping when I tell him. Darius is like an uncle to me. I've known him since I was six years old. He used to come with Malik to visit me at my foster parents' house.

"Hi, Raven, can I speak to Darius?"

I could hear Darius in the background telling Raven to say he wasn't in. *Damn, what's that all about?*

"Asia, he's not here. I thought he was in the pool with our son," said Raven.

"Oh, okay. Just tell him I called." I disconnected and stared at my cell phone, not believing what I just heard.

What's up with Darius? I need to talk to my brother and fast. I ain't leaving this hospital until I find out what's going on with him and Darius.

Chapter 18

Jamal

"Capri, you remember what you have to do on Friday?" I asked her.

"Yes, Mr. Long," said Capri, smiling and licking her lips.

"Do you always fuck every man that come up in your place?" I asked, straightening my clothes.

"Listen Jamal, it ain't like that. You lucky, you're cute and sexy—and on top of that my pussy was hot. I don't give up my pussy for free. So consider that a treat. "

"Whatever."

"You'll be back."

"For what?"

"Don't act like you don't know," she said, walking up on me.

"Gone girl," I smiled.

"See, you getting nervous already," she laughed.

"It ain't all that," I laughed in return.

"Oh, *really?*"

Before I could say another word, Capri pulled my pants back down, got on her knees, pulled my dick out and started licking around the tip of it. Ol' boy started rising. I tried to pull back, but it felt so damn good!

Damn, ol' girl know how to give helluva head. No wonder she was on her knees getting paid for this shit. I guess I am lucky.

"Oh, shittttt, Capri! *Capri!*" I hollered.

"Yeah, baby, you know my name," said Capri, continuing to lick and suck me dry.

"I gotta go. You trying to put a nigga out," I said, pulling up my pants.

"See you on Friday, partner" smiled Capri, licking her fingers

"Girl, your ass nasty!" I laughed again.

"You like this nasty girl?"

"Yeah, I do."

....

I left Capri's apartment with a big-ass smile on my face. *Damn, nigga, watch where you going!*

Gwen Cannon

I looked up, and there was John, standing in front of me in the parking lot.

"Nigga, what you doing over here?" asked John. He looked shocked to see me.

"Visiting a friend."

"Yeah, nigga, I knew it," smiled John.

"Knew what?"

"You and Capri."

"What about me and Capri?" I asked, trying not to show any emotion.

"I knew you were fucking her. Come on, man, you can tell me."

"We ain't fucking—and what the fuck are *you* doing over here?"

"Nigga, I *live* here, on the third floor."

Now it was my turn to look shocked. *John and Capri live in the same apartment building. Something ain't adding up. I wonder what the fuck they were really talking about in the parking lot.*

"How long have you been living here?"

"Three years," John told me.

"Did you know Capri lived here?"

"Yeah, I helped her move in. She was struggling with some boxes, and I offered to help. She moved here the same week she started working at our company. At the time, I didn't know she would be working at the same place we did."

"Oh."

"So, y'all fucking, huh?" asked John, again

"Damn, man, didn't I tell your ass no? She told me she was selling a flat-screen tv. I wanted to see how it looked."

"You gone buy it?" asked John, cocking his head to the side, as if he didn't believe a word I was saying.

"I'm going to think about it."

"You want to come up for a beer? My girl gone to the mall shopping," said John.

"Naw, man, I got some business I need to take care of. Maybe next time."

"Okay, bet," said John, as he walked up to the apartment building.

Damn, that's fucked up. I'm going to be sure to ask Capri why she didn't tell me she knew John. Ol' girl is sneaky as hell.

Gwen Cannon

Chapter 19

Kesha

"Mom, where you at?" I hollered as I entered the house.

Maybe she's gone to the store again. I'm going to take a shower and relax. I can't remember the last time I came home and mom didn't have a man laid up in here.

I went to my room and started changing my clothes. I thought I heard someone in the other room. I called out to my mother again, but no answer, so I went to her room.

There on the floor lay my mother in a fetal position.

I shook her. No movement.

"Mom, mom, wake up" hollered Kesha

She can't be dead. She said she had four to six months. But I knew she was gone; she felt hard and cold. I don't know how long she had been that way. Even though we'd fought earlier, she seemed alright when I left. We made up and agreed on a fresh start to our relationship. I sat on the floor and laid my mother's head on my lap. I kept rubbing her hair, and the tears started flowing. I knew deep in my heart that I loved my mother, despite all the horrible things she'd done.

She's still my mom, my sister would tell me, *God only gives you one mother in life.* God says to honor thy mother and thy father. I didn't do those things. All I did was complain and argue with her about the different men she would bring home. *God, I'm asking you to forgive me now. I love my mother with all my heart and now you have called her home. I know she's in a better place.* I couldn't move from that spot; the pain I felt at that moment was unbearable. I wish I could take back all the evil things I said to her.

We have to remember that tomorrow is not promised to anyone. My mother's death is proof of that. I sat there in that spot, holding on to my mother. I started reciting a poem I wrote to her when I was nine years old.

Mother I'm calling out to you
Mother can you see me
I'm standing right here
I need your love and affection
To wipe away my tears
Mom can't you see me standing here
Calling out your name
You don't see my tears, like droplets of rain
I need my mother's touch to ease my pain
I'm calling out for your love
I'm calling out for your touch
I need you mom, more than ever
I need you, oh so much!

I wrote that poem after my father left. At that time I really needed the love of a mother, but she wasn't trying to see or hear anything I had to say. I was hurting so much after my father left. She was in her own world then. I guess reality hit her, that he wasn't coming back.

She tried to change her hoe-ish ways after he left, thinking that he might come back. But the phone didn't ring, and he didn't' come back knocking at the door. You never miss what you had until it's gone. I know my father was a good man. He took care of home, and

made sure me and my sister had everything.
God, if you're listening, take care of my momma.

Gwen Cannon

Chapter 20

Malik, Asia, and Darius

"Malik, wake up. Come on, big bro; I need you," said Asia. I could feel her caressing my hand.

"Asia…" I whispered.

"Come on, Malik!" cried Asia, happy to see me respond. "I knew they couldn't hold you down!"

"What happened?"

"You were in a car accident."

"I can't remember shit," I said, rubbing my forehead.

"You don't remember what happened?"

"No, the last thing I remember is dropping you off at the mall."

"And nothing else?"

"No. My legs are killing me." I felt for them.

"The Doctor had to put some pins in your legs; they took a bad beating in the crash. They wanted to amputate, but I said, "Hell naw. Y'all better do what you can to save my brother's legs!'"

"Thanks, baby girl. I'm glad you was looking out for your bro." I cracked a little smile. It was hard to smile, what with the pain in my legs.

....

"I called Darius," I told Malik, trying to gauge his reaction.

"He's probably taking care of some business for me."

"When was the last time you talked to Darius?"

"What day is it? Probably two days ago. I can't remember."

"Well, I want you to get some rest. I'll let Darius know you're awake," I told him, walking out of the room.

Damn, he don't remember shit. But something is going on, because Darius was telling his girl to say he wasn't' home. I don't know what happened, but I'm going to find out. I got Malik's phone. I'm going to call Darius from his phone.

....

"Hello?"

"Darius is that you?"

"Yeah, baby girl, what's up? Why you calling me from Malik's phone?" asked Darius, sounding hesitant.

"Have you talked to Malik?"

"No" Why?"

"He's in the hospital. He was in a car accident last night. He got hurt pretty bad. He has to go through therapy for his legs."

"Damn, that's fucked up. What happened with his legs?" asked Darius.

"They got banged up pretty bad. The Doctor was talking that amputation shit. I told him, "Hell naw, y'all better do what you gotta do to save his legs.'"

....

"Did he ask for me?" I asked Asia. *I need to find out how much she knows.*

"No, he don't remember shit about the accident. He said the last thing he remembered was dropping me off at the mall."

"Damn, I better go see him." *That's a break for me: he lost part of memory.*

Now I need to go and see if Malik remembers anything about the transaction. Hell, I couldn't just let ol' boy hand over that much money. I need that to get the fuck up out of Detroit, and, if everything goes as planned, I'm going to be a rich motherfucka. I guess I can take Raven with me.

She's been down with me from day one, when I first started selling drugs. I remember her ass came up the block strutting around in some little-bitty-ass booty shorts. I smacked the shit out of her ass when she walked past. I thought she was gone just cuss my ass out for smacking her ass.

Ol' girl knocked the shit out of me; that shit was funny as hell. I couldn't believe she hit me. Normally, I would have beat the shit out of her, but it was something about her that made me change my mind. I knew then that I wanted her. I needed somebody like that who had some back. Someone who wouldn't let a nigga just run all over her, I needed that ride-or-die bitch by my side.

Damn, I better make my way over to Riverside hospital before visiting hours are over.

Gwen Cannon

Chapter 21

Raheem and Nina

"Nina, baby, bring me a beer" I hollered from the living room.

"Get your lazy ass up and get it yourself," she screamed from the bathroom.

"Damn, don't you love your man?"

"Yes, but I'm still not getting you a beer. You're closer to the kitchen then I am. Get your ass up!"

"Damn, I guess your ass ain't gone get it." I got mine off the couch.

As I walked back to the living room, swigging from the bottle, there was Nina, prancing around with a black teddy on. I almost choked on my beer when I saw her.

"Damn baby, you put that on for me?" I smiled, grabbing my crotch.

"No, I put this on for my boo. Who promised to take me out to dinner and to the club. Do you know him?" asked Nina, smiling.

"Yeah, baby. Come on over here. I know your boo," I smiled, licking my lips.

....

I started dancing around the room, like an exotic dancer. I knew what I was doing, and I knew exactly what Raheem liked. He loved to go to the strip club. Without Raheem knowing, I'd started taking classes for pole dancing.

I figured, if I learned how to dance like the strippers, maybe I could get in more quality time with him. The shit worked, because the first time I danced for him and did a strip tease, he didn't want to leave. Raheem first accused me of being a stripper on the side. Until I took him to the studio where I'd learned to pole dance.

Raheem pulled at the teddy. He could see that I didn't have any underwear on. I pushed him back and continued dancing. I was doing full splits, kicking my legs up in the air. Raheem couldn't' take anymore, he jumped up from the couch, grabbed me around the waist, and pulled me down on the couch. Gently, he

Gwen Cannon

put my legs around his neck and started licking my pussy.

I started jerking and moaning to the rhythm of his tongue. I knew his dick was rising to the occasion; he got up and plunged it so hard into me that I screamed. But his erotic smooth rhythm soon turned my screams into moans of pleasure.

"Fuck me; fuck me, baby! Yes, like that. Harder, *harder!* Damn, your dick feel so good!"

"You coming, baby, you coming?" moaned Raheem.

"Oh, oh, oooooooohhhhhhhhhhh, yes, yesss!" I screamed. And I did.

....

"Damn, baby, you funny as hell when you about to bust a nut," I laughed, lying there next to her.

"Shit, I can't help it. That shit felt good," said Nina, trying to catch her breath.

I knew how to please all my women, and Nina was number one on my list. She was smart, cute, with a tight-ass body, good-ass job, and A-1 credit. Those were the top five requirements that I insisted my women have. But Nina was special. She didn't know about my other women. I told her they worked for me. Nina received most of my time, the others were just late-night booty calls, or if I needed some snatch to hold my stash.

I preferred to fuck with women when it came to handling product. I learned long ago that you couldn't trust a nigga when it came to drugs and money. Women were better. They think you're doing *them* a favor.

....

"Nina, your phone ringing," I hollered.

"I'm in the shower. Answer it." So I did.

"Is Nina there?" cried Kesha.

"What's wrong, Kee?" The way she sounded, I couldn't help being concerned.

"I need to talk to Nina now!" said Kesha.

"Nina, you better come to the phone. It's your sister, she sounds upset."

Nina came down, wrapping a towel around herself. "What's up, Kesha?"

I didn't hear what Kesha said, but I saw Nina just standing there, motionless, holding the phone, no words coming out of her mouth.

"Nina, are you alright?" I asked.

When she didn't reply, didn't move, I took the phone from her.

"Kesha, what's going on? Nina's standing here ain't saying shit. What happened?"

"Momma's dead!" wailed Kesha.

"Damn, I'm sorry. What happened?"

"She had a brain tumor. The doctors gave her four to six months, but I guess they didn't know what the fuck they were talking about," cried Kesha.

"We'll be right there," I told her.

I helped Nina get dressed. I had never seen her like this before. She was in a daze; she didn't utter a word the whole ride to her mother's house.

Chapter 22

Jamal, Capri, and Mr. Cain

"Capri, you ready?"

"Yeah, nigga. I told you: I got this," said Capri.

"Okay. He's about to come in my office now."

"What's so important that it couldn't wait, Jamal?" asked Mr. Cain. He was always acting like he had somewhere more important to be. I guess that's the way you have to act if you're a boss.

"I got something you should see," I explained.

"What? I haven't got all day."

Out of the closet walked Capri, smiling. She handed Mr. Cain an envelope and a videotape.

"What's going on?" asked Mr. Cain, as if he didn't know. He was starting to sweat.

"I have a proposition for you," I told him.

"What's this all about?" hollered Mr. Cain.

"Please, Mr. Cain, let's be calm about this. Please take a look at the contents of the envelope and the videotape," I said smoothly, as if we were was having a business meeting.

Mr. Cain opened the envelope and started looking at the many picture. Then he came across some budget reports and data that contained what the company should have generated in profits for the year. Mr. Cain's hand started shaking; sweat dripped from his forehead.

"Jamal, what are you doing with this report. I'm the only one who is supposed to get a copy of this," said Mr. Cain nervously.

"Mr. Cain, you and I know what has been going on for the last four years. You got greedy with your father-in-law's company. See, just like you've been watching me, I've been watching you. I knew you were trying to get rid of me once you knew that your secretary gave me your reports by mistake. I looked them over and saw that you were taking a big chunk of the company's profit every quarter. I was smart enough to make copies, Mr. Cain. Now you have the videotape, which has clips of you and various women fucking in your office. I know you don't want that to get in Mrs. Cain's hands." I couldn't help smirking, just a little.

By now, Mr. Cain was dripping with perspiration. He looked like he was about to have a heart attack.

"Mr. Cain, we can settle this now. All you have to do is put $250,000 in my account by the end of the day."

....

I felt my eyes widen when Jamal said "$250,000." He told me that he was going to ask for $100,000 and give me 40% of the money. Maybe he forgot what he'd said—or he was trying to play me. I knew when someone was trying to play me. Either way, I was going to get my 40% of whatever amount Jamal was getting.

....

I told Jamal I would have an answer for him by the end of the day. "I don't have that kind of money just sitting around, you know." I left Jamal's office in a sweat, feeling delirious. My heart felt like it was about to explode.

I knew for a fact I didn't have $250,000, but I wasn't going to tell Jamal that. I kept pacing around my office, wiping my forehead. I knew there was only one thing that would resolve this mess I had gotten myself into. I wished I could turn the clocks back so that this never had happened, but it was done now, so I was going to have to do what I thought was best for everyone.

I sat at my desk, with the lights off, my face expressionless. I said a silent prayer, asking God to forgive me for my sins. I left my wife a long voice message, apologizing, telling her I loved her. I straightened my tie, buttoned up my jacket, and got up from my desk.

....

Jamal reclined back in his chair, with a big-ass smile across his face. Thinking about his big pay day.

"Jamal, you lied," I told him, standing in front of him with my hands on my hips.

"No, I just asked for more money," said Jamal smiling.

"Shit, that's what I'm talking about! Make that motherfucka pay!" I said, doing a little dance around Jamal's office.

There was some commotion in the outer office. Jamal opened his office door. We could see the other employees running around the office, shouting, "He has a gun!"

Jamal saw Mr. Cain coming, looking like a mad man. Before he could get the door closed, Mr. Cain charged into his office. He started shooting. I started screaming.

....

"Good evening, ladies and gentlemen. This is Carmen Goodall, Local 4 News.

"Tragedy struck Cain Enterprises today. According to eyewitnesses, the company's owner and CEO went on a rampage.

"When the commotion ended, three people were announced dead at the scene.

"Jamal Long, Capri Thomas, and Mr. Cain himself."

Chapter 23

Kesha

We sat around the kitchen table making arrangements for momma's funeral. Nina still didn't seem like she was capable of making any type of decisions. She cried all day long. We had to medicate her to calm her down. I never thought she would take it like that.

I had to be the head of the house now. My father helped out a lot; he insisted on paying for everything. I was proud that he stood up and made sure everything was in place. He said he still loved my mother, but he was not in love with her. He said she gave him two beautiful daughters.

The day of the funeral, it rained all day long. I think that was the saddest day of my life, apart from the day my father walked out on us.

I didn't realize so many people actually liked my mother until the day of the funeral. The church was standing room only. So many strangers came up to me to give their condolences.

I wrote a poem the day of my mother's funeral. Because her death was unexpected, I wrote a poem about Life and Death. I didn't know if I would be able to hold up and read it aloud, but I prayed to God to give me strength and I read what was my last dedication to my mother.

Life and Death

We never see it coming; we never really knew. Our life gets taken from us, sometimes right out of the blue.

No one ever wants to die; death is a scary thing. We wonder will we go to heaven or hell; no one knows what death may bring.

Cherish your todays; cherish your tomorrows; life brings many things, like happiness and sorrow.

Gwen Cannon

Live your life to the fullest, always treat others with respect. God and the Red Demon are watching who to bring to their nest.
Life is a blessing, and death is a part of life. Look at life as a stepping stone of wisdom and knowledge; look at death as the next step after life into the unknown.
Always think about how you've lived your life. Will I go to heaven or take that drop down to hell? No one really knows, only God can tell.

After the funeral, my father, Nina, and I sat in the living room trying to decide what to do with the house. My father had paid cash for it. When he and my mother first met, this crack-head who was strung out bad sold the house to my father for $3,000. It wasn't the best house, but it was paid for.

We had a realtor put the house on the market. The realtor advised us that we probably could get $25,000 for it.

We decided that, whatever money we received, would be split between me and Nina. My father said that was the least he could do. Nina insisted that I come stay with her. She was really feeling depressed, and having someone at home with her would help. I accepted her offer, packed my bags, and we were on our way to my new home.

We told our father we would visit for the holidays. He was happy to hear that; now we would get to meet our extended family. *I just hope me moving in with Nina, doesn't cause any problems between her and Raheem. Time will tell.*

Chapter 24

Malik

I lay in the hospital bed with my eyes closed, listening to everyone around me. I knew, if I act as if I'd lost my memory, Darius' dumb ass would definitely try and make his way up to the hospital. The only pain I felt was in my legs, although my head was throbbing a little from the impact on the dash board. I felt blessed to be alive. But I knew I had better move fast.

After Asia left, I immediately put in a phone call to one of the boys from back in the day—nigga named Butch. Butch was a crazy motherfucka who would kill his mother if he had to. When I gave Butch the low down about Darius, he was ready to do whatever I needed him to do. But I told Butch I wanted to handle this one on my own. I gave Butch a little list and had him bring me everything on it. I just had to put my plan in motion.

I advised the nurse's station that I didn't want any visitors for the remainder of the day, that I wanted to rest. Since Asia was gone for the day, it gave me time to put my plan in place. I decided to call Raheem. Raheem would help me out.

....

"Raheem, you busy?"

"Not really, I'm at my girl's house, waiting for her to get home. Her mother's funeral was today. I didn't want to hang around, so I came back to the house. What up?"

"I'm sorry to hear about your girl's mother. You have my condolences."

"Thanks, man."

"I'm at Riverside hospital. I'm going to need your help with something. I don't want to talk over the phone. Come by tomorrow around 2:00 p.m. We can talk then. —Oh, if you happen to run into Darius, act like you don't know shit."

"Bet," said Raheem. "See you tomorrow."

Just then, the nurse stuck her head in the door and said, "Mr. Waters, a gentleman came by to see you, I informed him that you were resting and to come back tomorrow."

"Did he leave his name?"

"No."

"Well, thank you, nurse."

So this motherfucka had the audacity to come to the hospital. I know he's wondering what's up with me. He's gone wish he never took shit from me after I'm finished with him. This motherfucka gone pay big time.

Chapter 25

Raheem

I opened the door for Nina and Kesha when I saw them walking up the driveway.

"Hey baby, you alright? Can I get you anything?" I asked Nina, concerned.

"No, I'm okay," Nina claimed.

I noticed the two suitcases Kesha was carrying. I didn't want to question Nina in front of Kesha, so I kept my thoughts to myself for the time being. *Damn, I hope Kesha ain't moving in. Hopefully she's just coming over for a few days. I'll check this out with Nina later. I need to check in with my brother, I wonder how that shit went down today. Damn, his phone is going to voice mail, I'll call his crib.*

Ebony answered on the second ring.

"Ebony, is Jamal home?"

"No, I haven't seen him since this morning when I left for my doctor's appointment."

"When he gets in, tell him to call me."

"Okay."

Damn, I wonder where the fuck he's at. He get off work at 5:00; it's after 6:00 now. I'm going to ride by his crib on my way to my place. I don't know why I pay rent at an apartment I'm barely at. I'm always at Nina's. I was thinking about moving in with her, but, seeing Kesha with suitcases I might have to wait on that.

....

As soon as I walked in the house and plopped my ass on her sofa, I asked Ebony, "Jamal made it home yet?"

"Naw, he might be at one of them skank-ass hoes' houses," said Ebony.

"How you know where he might be at—you following him ?" I asked, laughing.

"Hell naw. Why would I be following your brother? I ain't no fucking stalker," said Ebony, looking at me like I was crazy

"You know you still got the hots for Jamal. You just chose my other brother Chuck 'cause he soft."

"Whatever, Raheem," said Ebony, turning up her nose and taking her snooty ass into the other room.

There was a knock at the door.

"Ebony, somebody's at the door," I hollered.

"Damn, you can answer it; you're right there!" shouted Ebony.

I made my way over to the door. "Who is it?"

"Detective Smith."

Why the fuck is a detective at the door? I got nervous and asked, "Who are you looking for?"

"Are you related to Jamal Long?" asked the detective.

"Yes, I'm his brother."

"Sir, can you please open the door? I have a few questions I want to ask you about your brother," said the detective.

Wondering if this had anything to do with what Jamal had planned for today, I opened the door and asked the detective what the problem was.

....

I waited 'til I could see his face before I told him. "I'm sorry, but your brother was shot and killed today at his job," said the detective. I wanted to see his reaction.

....

I looked at the detective like he was crazy. "What did you just say?"

"Your brother, along with two other victims, was shot and killed. It looks like the owner shot your brother and a female co-worker and then turned the gun on himself."

"What female?" I asked, still in shock.

"She went by the name Capri Thomas, but her legal name was Tia Jones. She used various aliases; she knew the Feds were onto her. She even tried to change her appearance. It looks like your brother got caught in the middle of a deal gone bad between Ms. Jones and Mr. Cain. We found photos and video of her and Mr. Cain performing sexual acts. It looks like she was probably trying to blackmail him for money. I think your brother got caught in the line of fire.

"Look, I see that you're upset, Mr. Long. When you get a chance, we would like for you to come down to the station. I still have some questions I would like to ask you."

....

The detective knew who Raheem Long was. He had heard about his dealing with the law and drugs.

I've got a hunch that his brother Jamal had something to do with what happened. "See you at the station, Mr. Long. You have my condolences."

....

Raheem stood in the doorway of the house looking up toward the sky. Tears were running down his face. His jaws were tight, his fists clenched. He now knew what it felt like to lose someone you love.

Gwen Cannon

Chapter 26

Kesha and Nina

"Nina, I wanted to say thanks again for letting me stay with you. You don't know how much this means to me," I said, hugging Nina.

"You're my sister, Kesha. You're family, and family comes first," said Nina.

"I don't want to cause any friction between you and Raheem. You know he really doesn't care for me."

"Raheem will be alright. He said you got a smart-ass mouth—and you certainly do," said Nina, smiling.

"It's just that I know you can do better. You're smart and beautiful—yet you're with Raheem. He don't have shit, but drug money. I just don't want to see you get hurt, that's all," I said, showing my concern.

"My little sister looking out for her big sister! I appreciate that. But I can handle Raheem; don't' worry about that," said Nina.

"Ok, you're the HBIC," I said, laughing.

"Oh, you got jokes now, huh?" asked Nina.

"But, seriously, big sis, what do you look for in a good man? Let me rephrase that—what do you look for in a black man?"

"I guess, someone who's caring, a gentleman, someone who can take control of a situation and definitely have a little thug in them," said Nina smiling.

"Well, I wrote a poem for you, and it's about the black man."

"Your ass always walking around with that notebook, writing poetry. You should really think about getting your poems published; you definitely be writing some deep shit," Nina told me.

"I express my feeling through my poetry."

"Okay, let me hear what you have to say about the black man, since you wrote it for me."

Black Man, Black Man

Black man, black man, oh how we love the
different shades you come in.
Chocolate like cocoa, or vanilla ice cream, what
about carmel, that's the man of my dreams.
Afro, bald, or even a tight fade,
What do you prefer? We don't care—
We just want to get laid!
What do we look for in the black man?
Someone who can take control, someone who
can take a stand.
Someone who's strong, with a gentle touch, he
can make you moan and desire him oh so much.
This man of many colors makes me lose all track
of time. I can't function at work; I can't get him off
my mind.
From last night's creep, to this morning's wake-
me-up,
Just to feel his skin on mine, and the way he
caresses my butt.
He's yours for the keeping, if you know what I
mean. Just put that sumpin, sumpin on him; put
him to sleep, make him have a wet dream.
Trust me he won't forget you, not after last
night. He may try to stray away; he may try to put
up a fight.

The blood hound in him won't let him stray too long; he'll sniff you out, he'll find his way back home.

But, just keep in mind, Nina, you're the one in control; just put a beer in one hand, and the other the remote control.

"Damn, Kesha, that shit was deep. How the hell you be coming up with that?" Said Nina, laughing.

"I don't know, I just put words with what I see and feel," Happy to hear her praise.

"You're still a virgin, and you writing how a nigga caresses your butt," laughed Nina.

"Whatever. I might be a virgin, but I know what be going on. Shit, I ain't stupid," I said, laughing in turn.

I loved when I could have a decent conversation with Nina and no arguing was involved. I just wanted Nina to be happy. Now that our mother was at peace, I wanted to concentrate on finishing school and getting the hell out of Detroit. I couldn't wait.

"Kesha, you want to go get something to eat?"

"That sounds good. I'm starved."

"I'm going to call Raheem and see if he wants to join us," said Nina.

Damn, I thought it would just be me and Nina. —But I doubt if Raheem will go once he finds out I'm going.

....

"Raheem, pick up the damn phone."

I hate that shit when he doesn't pick up, I know he hears his phone ringing. Oh, well, I guess it'll be just me and Kesha going out to eat. I'm starved, I haven't eaten anything since yesterday morning. I really haven't had an appetite since Mom died. I'm going to miss her.

"Kesha, you ready?"

"Yeah, let's go," said Kesha, coming down the stairs.

....

On the way to the restaurant, I felt like confessing for some reason. I had been holding onto some information I had found out two weeks ago but didn't know how to go about telling Raheem. It was eating me up because I hadn't told anyone.

I found out I was pregnant when I went in for my annual physical. I hadn't told anyone, because I didn't know if I wanted to keep the baby or not. Raheem was always saying he didn't want to bring any kids into this fucked-up world. So I had to make a decision. Telling

Kesha would get this off my chest; I had to tell someone—and who better than my sister?

"Kesha, I have something I want to tell you. Please don't judge me after you hear it. I've been holding this in for the last two weeks. Now I wish I would have told momma. I know she would have been happy."

"What the hell are you talking about?" asked Kesha.

I looked at Kesha, smiling, and put my hand on my belly.

"Why are you smiling and shit, and rubbing your stomach? Please keep your eyes on the traffic. I already know what you're about to say," said Kesha.

"What?"

"You're pregnant."

"How the hell did you know?"

"Well, I'm not going to tell a lie. I saw the pregnancy test in your garbage outside about two weeks ago."

"Your ass, digging through my old trash? I took the test because I thought the doctor could be wrong. But I guess not."

"I was looking for my bracelet. I lost it, and I thought maybe I dropped it in your trash when I took it out to the dumpster for you."

"Why didn't you say something then?"

"I was hoping it wasn't true."

"Why?" I asked, looking at Kesha, concerned.

"You know how I feel about Raheem."

"I know y'all don't like each other…"

"He's okay, but you can do better."

"Well, he's the daddy. I didn't know if I wanted to be tied down with a baby right now, but, after mom's death, I changed my mind. I know she would have wanted me to keep the baby."

"Yeah, she kept asking when you were going to make her a grandma. So, when are you going to tell Raheem?"

"I don't know."

"What are you waiting for?"

"I was going to tell him today, but he's not answering his phone. I'll try calling him again."

....

"Hello?"

"Raheem, is that you?"

"Yeah," said Raheem, sounding distant. I thought it was a bad connection.

"What's wrong? You sound upset."

"My brother's dead," said Raheem.

I felt sure it was a bad connection. "What did you say?"

"My brother Jamal is *dead*."

"Oh, baby, I'm on my way. Where are you?"

"At Jamal's house: 21456 Parklane Drive."

"Raheem, I'll be there in fifteen minutes" I said, hanging up the phone

"What happened?" asked Kesha.

"Raheem's brother Jamal is dead."

"*What?* That's fucked up! He was so cool."

"You knew Raheem's brother?"

"Yeah, he was straight. One of the good guys," said Kesha with sincerity.

I was dodging in and out of traffic, trying to get to Raheem. I didn't think now would be the right time to spring my pregnancy on him. That's probably the last thing he would want to hear. I decided to hold off.

Gwen Cannon

Chapter 27

Malik, Asia, and Raheem

I *better check on Asia and see what time she's trying to come up here. I don't want her caught up in this shit.*

"Asia, when are you planning on coming up here?"

"Why, you got somewhere to go?" laughed Asia.

"Oh, you funny, huh?"

"Damn, you sound good. What the hell did they give you? Your ass was knocked the fuck out when I left yesterday," said Asia.

"I'm straight—just a little sore."

"I'll probably stop by about 1:30," said Asia.

"Why don't you come earlier?—make it 11:30 in the morning."

"Why so early?"

"They want to run some tests. I think the nurse said between 1:00 and 3:00."

"Okay, then I'll see you at 11:30." said Asia.

....

I didn't believe a word Malik said. I knew he was up to something. I definitely didn't believe him about taking some tests. I decided to go to the hospital at 11:30, and hang around afterwards in the hospital cafeteria.

My gut feeling was telling me something was about to jump off. Especially after the shit with Darius, when I called him the other night. I knew, if I asked Malik about it, he would make something up. He always told me he didn't want me involved in any of his business.

....

I hope Raheem remembers to come by today at 2:00. I need to have this shit in place in case that dirty motherfucka Darius shows up. I know his lazy ass isn't going to try and come early. He's not an early riser; his ass gets up around 1:00 p.m. That's why, when Raheem told me Darius woke him up early about the money, I knew he wasn't lying. That shit still got me fucked up. Life's a bitch.

....

"Raheem, don't forget to come by the hospital at 2:00," said Malik into the phone.

"Yeah, man."

"Man, you okay? You sound like you got fucked up last night," said Malik.

"Naw, dog, I went out with my girl. We got in late."

"You sure, you okay?"

"Yeah, I'll be there," I assured him and hung up the phone.

I didn't want to talk about Jamal's death. I was still fucked up about it. I couldn't understand what could have possibly happened to make Mr. Cain shoot Jamal, Capri, and himself.

I guess his ass couldn't take it. Damn, I wish I would have never gave Jamal that shit now. He would probably still be alive. I feel like his death was my fault. I'm going to have to live with this shit for the rest of my life.

Chapter 28

Raheem

"Nina, I got to go take care of some business."

"Baby, you sure you gone be alright? I can go with you," said Nina.

"I'm straight, I have to go down to the police station first. They have some questions to ask me about Jamal."

"What questions?"

"I don't know. His co-worker got caught up in some scandalous shit with their boss."

"Call me if you need anything," said Nina.

"Okay,"

I was still trying to figure out what happened with Jamal. The plan he'd laid out seemed fool proof. *Ol' girl must have had something to do with the fuck-up. I'll see what the detective has to say.*

When I walked into the police station, it seemed like every cop in the place knew who I was. They were whispering and eye balling me.

"I'm here to see Detective Smith," I told the desk sergeant.

"Wait here, I'll get him."

I hated being in a police station; it brought back bad memories. One of my partners got killed in lock up at the police station. They put on his death certificate suicide by hanging. But I knew one of the cops had something to do with his murder.

"Mr. Long, you can step into my office? Right this way," said Detective Smith, pointing to his office.

"What can I do for you?"

"I just need to ask you a few questions"

"Okay, shoot. —Pardon the expression."

"What was your brother's relationship with Tia Jones?"

"Sir, I don't know who Tia Jones is."

"Well, we have a witness who states that they were in a relationship."

"What witness?"

"Ebony Woods was here earlier today. She was really upset about your brother's death. What was your brother and Ebony's relationship?"

"Ebony is pregnant by my brother Chuck. He's in basic training." *Why the fuck did Ebony come down to the precinct?*

"Well, she was really shook up over your brother's death. We had to call a medic to calm her down," said the detective.

"Look, Detective Smith, I don't know Tia Jones and my brother didn't have any type of relationship with Ebony. I told you, she was pregnant by my brother Chuck." I was getting angry.

"Well, thanks for coming down. I'll be talking to you again." He said it with a smirk on his face.

I don't know what the fuck he smiling about. That motherfucka ain't gone see me again. I need to go find out what the fuck Ebony's ass was down here saying.

....

"Ebony, where the fuck you at?" I hollered, walking into the house.

"Damn, you could knock!" shouted Ebony from upstairs.

"My brother left me a key, so I don't have to fucking knock. Just get your ass down stairs; we need to talk."

....

Raheem's tone made me nervous. But, before the motherfucka could ask me a thousand damn questions, I came right out and told him: "Yeah, I told the detective about Jamal and that bitch. I followed his ass to her house the other day.

"I stood there outside her window and saw everything. Her hoe-ish ass strutting around in a tank top and thong. She knew what the fuck she was doing. I couldn't believe Jamal fell for that shit. Then this nigga gone fuck her. Hell yeah, I told the detective everything, and I don't regret the shit." Then I started crying— hard.

I still had feelings for Jamal; I guess I thought that, after the other day when we had sex, there was a chance we could hook up.

I'm pregnant by Chuck, but my heart aches for Jamal. When I heard he was dead, I didn't give a fuck who knew we had made love. I was tore up inside, I couldn't stop crying that night, like I can't stop cryinig now.

I know Raheem was tripping, the way he was staring at me when I broke down. He just stood there with this look on his face, like he knew what had happened between me and Jamal. Before he left out the door, he called me a Scandalous Bitch.

Chapter 29

Kesha and Raheem

"Nina, I don't want to be a burden on you and your relationship with Raheem. I'm going to find me a job and get me an apartment."

"You know you can't afford an apartment," said Nina.

"I know, but I feel bad. You're pregnant now, and you don't need me in the way."

"What do you mean, 'in the way'? You're my little sister, and I love you. I'm going to make sure you're alright. That's the least I can do. We'll sell the house and go from there. Let's just take it one day at a time," said Nina.

"Okay—but let me know if I'm getting on your nerves. You're pregnant now and I know your hormones are going to make you a real bitch," I laughed.

"Oh, you got jokes now, huh?" smiled Nina.

"I am excited: I'm going to be an auntie," I announced, dancing around the kitchen.

"Yeah, Auntie Kesha."

"I know mom would have been excited."

"Yeah, if it's a girl, I'm going to give her mom's middle name. Tamika."

"Can I give her a nickname?"

"Yeah, I guess so…"

"What about Tee-Tee?"

"I don't know about Tee-Tee. I had this girl in my class. They called her Tee-Tee. I *hated* her!" laughed Nina.

....

We had a long sister–to-sister conversation about life in general and our plans for the future. The best part was my pregnancy. We both were excited, but Raheem still didn't know, and I was wondering when would be a good time to tell him. I didn't want to put any more burdens on him then he already had.

I would just have to wait for the right time. I told Kesha to make herself at home. This was her home now. I took her shopping for new clothes to start school next week. It

Gwen Cannon

was so much fun—Kesha was so excited; she hadn't been shopping in years. So I took her to get her hair and nails done. Kesha got her hair cut into a cute short bob.

Kesha couldn't wait to show off her new hairdo and clothes. When we got home, Kesha insisted on cooking dinner. I didn't resist; I was tired from all the running around. I guess the baby was starting to tire me out. And I was really worried about Raheem; I hadn't heard from him since early this morning when he left. I decided to call him.

....

"Raheem, are you alright? I was worried about you. I haven't heard from you all day," said Nina

"I'm straight; I'm at my brother's house."

"What time are you coming over?"

"I don't know. I have another stop to make when I leave here."

"Be careful, baby," said Nina.

"I'm straight," I repeated.

"I'll see you later, then," said Nina.

"Bet," I told her and hung up.

I didn't feel like hearing Ebony lie about herself and Jamal, so I'd left. I was still trying to figure out what could have happened with Jamal's plan. Obviously it backfired, but I didn't think anyone would get killed in the process. I was learning real quick that the scandalous shit you do can bite the shit outta your ass. It killed my brother.

I looked at my watch and saw that it was getting close to 2:00 p.m. I decided to make my way over to the hospital to see Malik.

Chapter 30

Malik

*I*t's almost 2:00; Raheem should be here soon. Darius is going to be in for a fucking surprise when he comes. I know he's going to make his way up; that's why I had to be sure. I called his girl, Raven and left a message that the nurse told me he had come by. I told her to tell Darius to come today and to bring me something to eat. I didn't want to give that nigga no clue that I knew what happened.

My little sister was asking a whole lot of damn questions when she was here. I know she's just worried about me. I think I'm going to take her on a long vacation when I get up out of here.

"Mr. Waters, you have a visitor," the nurse said: "Mr. Raheem Long."

"Okay, send him in, please."

Raheem came in smiling. "What up, nigga?"

"Nothing, just trying to heal, man. You okay? I wanted to send flowers for your brother. Make sure you give me the address of the funeral home."

"Thanks, man, I appreciate that," said Raheem, giving Malik dap.

"We need to get down to business."

"I'm down with whatever."

Raheem seemed to have an "I-don't-give-a–fuck" attitude since his brother's death.

I gave Raheem all the pertinent details of what was going to transpire when Darius showed up. We had everything in place; it was just a matter of time now.

....

Big brother didn't know that I had snuck back in his room and was hiding in the bathroom listening to everything him and Raheem planned to do.

When I heard Raheem's name, I knew who he was; he used to try and talk to me. But, when he found out Malik was my brother, he left me alone. I knew Nina was Raheem's woman; I found that out from Malik's conversation with Darius at the house one day. I scrolled through my cell phone, trying to locate Kesha's number. I was hoping Kesha still had the same number, I hadn't talked to Kesha in a while. Once I found Kesha's number, I immediately dialed it.

"Please be the same number," I whispered as the phone was ringing

It was. "Hello," said Kesha.

"Kesha, this is Asia. I don't know if you remember me—"

....

"Hey, girl, I remember you. You still singing?" I asked, wondering why Asia was calling her.

"Yeah, but I don't want to hold you long. I have an emergency situation."

"What emergency?"

Asia gave me all the details of what her brother and Raheem were planning to do to Darius. I couldn't believe what was about to happen. I didn't want to get Nina upset in her condition, so I decided against telling her. I made up some story and asked Nina if I could go visit my friend Jazmine, who I hadn't seen or talked to her since momma had passed.

I left the house with one of Raheem's guns stashed in my book bag.

Chapter 31

Asia and Kesha

I met Kesha outside in the hospital parking lot, then took her up to the floor where Malik's room was. We decided to hide in the room next to Malik's since no one was occupying it. We waited until we heard the nurse announcing a visitor for Mr. Waters. I peeped my head in the hallway to see who it was.

Darius and Raven were coming down the hospital corridor. Darius had a McDonald's bag in his hand. *Damn, I didn't know Raven was coming with him. Shit I hope she don't get hurt in the process.* I thought about telling them not to go in the room, but decided against it. I didn't want Malik to know I knew what was about to jump off.

Darius and Raven made their way to Malik's room. I could hear Malik talking to Darius.

He was telling Darius he needed to talk to him in private, but Darius kept insisting that whatever he had to say he could say in front of Raven. Raven wasn't aware of what was going on and told Darius that it was alright, that she would wait in the hallway. Me and Kesha felt better when we saw Raven come out of the room and shut the door behind her. All of a sudden, all you could hear was shouting and cussing.

Three different voices shouting and cussing.

....

"Darius, I thought you would never do something like this to me!" Malik shouted.

"Nigga, whatever. You was going around bragging to niggas that you was about to get out of the game and just leave me hanging. Shit, I was thinking about my future." He advanced on Malik, menacingly. Malik could only lay there and watch him.

That's when Raheem sprang up. "Hold on, motherfucka!" I hollered, coming up from the other side of the room. I held a gun to Darius' head.

"Oh, you gone play me like this? Bring this nigga on board?" Darius tried to play hard.

"Naw, he didn't bring me on board," I said. "But I told him I would help put your ass out. You broke the first rule of the drug game: never play your partner."

Before anyone could say another word, Darius reached in the back of his pants. I instantly pulled the trigger and put two shots in Darius' head, not knowing that Darius was reaching in his back pocket for paper work showing where he had deposited all the money in an account for Malik. He had realized that their friendship was worth more than the money. Malik's door flew open; someone came running in.

I didn't stop to look and see who it was— my reflexes took over. I blasted two more shots.

Asia lay on the floor with one gun shot to her chest and one in her stomach.

....

Kesha stood in the doorway in shock; she couldn't move. Nurses and doctors were running around, trying to save Asia and Darius. The defibrillator was brought in.

Malik sat there with tears streaming down his face, watching his sister's chest pop up and down from the machine they were using. They had never heard a man scream like Malik was screaming. The echo of his screams could be heard throughout the hospital. All he was saying was "Asia..., Asia..., Asia...!"

Raven stepped around me and came into the room, crying, pulling at Darius on the floor. She stared up at Malik and Raheem with a look of hatred and revenge. She reached in her purse. More gunshots rang out in the room.

Once the commotion died down, Malik lay in his bed with a bullet to the head, and Raheem lay on the floor grasping his chest and coughing up blood. One of the doctors grabbed the gun out of Raven's hand. She just stood there in a daze, as if she didn't know what just happened.

....

I turned on the 5:00 news with Carmen Goodall. *I probably shouldn't be watching any of this upsetting shit, what with the baby coming and all, but there's nothing else on tv—and how bad can it be?*

I found out. I fell to the floor when I saw Raheem's face come across the screen. Above my wails, I could hear the newscaster announce that "Malik Waters, known drug dealer, was killed in his hospital bed. His sister, Asia Waters, was shot and killed. Darius Moore, known drug dealer, was also killed. Raheem Long is listed in critical condition with a gunshot wound to the chest."

Chapter 32

Conclusion

There was a total of six funerals within two weeks. Nina and Kesha attended Asia's funeral. It was a double funeral for Asia and Malik. Asia's foster parents thought she would have wanted it that way. They knew how much Asia loved her brother.

Chuck was released from basic training to attend Jamal's funeral. He couldn't understand why Ebony was taking it so hard. She had to be carried out of the church.

Raheem remained in critical condition at Riverside hospital under 24-hour police watch until he was strong enough to go to jail and await trial for the shooting deaths of Darius and Asia.

When the police arrived at the hospital, Raven was babbling incessantly, smiling ghoulishly and repeating the same phrase over and over again: "revenge is a motherfucka; revenge is a motherfucka; revenge-is-a-motherfucka." The doctors had her admitted to a mental institution.

Kesha and Nina left Detroit and went to live closer to their father in Toledo, Ohio. Nina lost the baby the night of the shooting. The stress brought on by the shooting caused her to miscarry. Kesha vowed to never date a drug dealer.

No one attended the funeral of Capri, aka Tia Jones–except for one person. He knew all about Capri and Jamal's plan. He wrote a letter addressed to Raheem at the hospital, vowing to avenge his sister's death. The letter stated that his sister left a package which contained everything that was to take place between Jamal and Mr. Cain. Since Jamal was dead, the next of kin would have to do. Either Raheem or Chuck. He concluded the letter,

Life's a bitch, and revenge is a motherfucka,
Signed by the motherfucka coming for you!!

John Jones

Gwen Cannon

John knew all about his sister's scandalous past—writing bad checks, committing credit-card fraud, and robbing niggas. Once he knew Mr. Cain was trying to fire Jamal, he brought his sister, Capri, into the company. He had her go into Jamal's office to see if she could find anything on the computer or inside his desk. That's when Jamal noticed that someone had been in his office.

John knew his sister would come up with a good-ass lie to tell Jamal. No one knew that John was Capri's brother. They had put together their own plan to blackmail Mr. Cain, but, when Jamal approached Capri, his plan sounded better, and John told her to play along with Jamal. They had planned to take the money and leave Jamal hanging, but the shit backfired. That scandalous shit we do comes back to bite us in the ass.